'Plenty man getting nicked all over town, Billy,' said Lynden. 'If I didn't know yer and I heard you asking all these questions – I'd think you was a grass.'

'You don't, do you?' I asked, worried for a moment. It wasn't even that I was *that* concerned about the dealers. I couldn't have cared less. They knew the risks before they started. I just didn't want my dad to think that I was a grass. Not my dad.

'Nah – I know you better than you think. Just mind who you ask questions. All it takes is one whisper in a man ear and the next thing you know, you got yourself a rep.'

I didn't know it then but by the time my dad had dropped me off outside my mum's house, things had already spun way out of our control. The whispers were about to become shouts . . .

Critical acclaim for *the crew*:
'Written in a streetwise dialect, this is a jewel of a book . . .' *Independent*

'Engagingly direct in tone, grittily realistic in theme, this uncompromising, streetwise story is sure to appeal' *Books for Keeps*

And for *Rani and Sukh*:
'Bali Rai speaks the voice of teenage youth with astonishing clarity' *Asiana*

'This powerful read is unforgettable, 5 stars out of 5' *Mizz*

Also available by Bali Rai,
and published by Corgi Books:

(un)arranged marriage
the crew
Rani and Sukh

bali rai
the whisper

corgi books

THE WHISPER

A CORGI BOOK 0 552 54891 X

Published in Great Britain by Corgi Books,
an imprint of Random House Children's Books

Corgi edition published 2005

1 3 5 7 9 10 8 6 4 2

Set in Bembo MT Schoolbook 12.5/15pt
by Falcon Oast Graphic Art Ltd.

Corgi Books are published by Random House Children's Books,
61–63 Uxbridge Road, London W5 5SA,
a division of The Random House Group Ltd,
in Australia by Random House Australia (Pty) Ltd,
20 Alfred Street, Milsons Point, Sydney, NSW 2061, Australia,
in New Zealand by Random House New Zealand Ltd,
18 Poland Road, Glenfield, Auckland 10, New Zealand,
and in South Africa by Random House (Pty) Ltd,
Endulini, 5A Jubilee Road, Parktown 2193, South Africa

THE RANDOM HOUSE GROUP Limited Reg. No. 954009
www.kidsatrandomhouse.co.uk

A CIP catalogue record for this book is available from the British Library.

Printed and bound in Great Britain by
Cox & Wyman Ltd, Reading, Berkshire.

This one is going out to all the readers all over the UK who asked me to write a sequel to *the crew*. I just hope that you like it as much.

And a special request to all reggae people all over the place, especially the artists who have made my aural world a paradise: people like Aba-Shanti-I sound, Jah Shaka, Dennis Brown, Augustus Pablo, The Wailers, Black Uhuru, UB40, Aswad, I-Roy, U-Roy, Big Youth, Jammy's, Sly and Robbie, Burning Spear, and all artists old and new (too many to mention). It was you I was listening to when I wrote these words . . .

And finally to all the young people in the UK excluded from the school system. Be strong, keep getting up when they knock you down and you will succeed. Wisdom is better than silver and gold . . .

ONE

'Come on, you stupid *shit*!'

Zeus, my lazy, dribbling Rottweiler, looked up at me through his watery eyes and made me feel guilty for swearing at him.

'I'm sorry,' I told him, in a whisper so that the two girls walking past us didn't hear me and think that I was off my head. Zeus padded forward for about thirty seconds before stopping again.

'*Zeus!*'

'That t'ing too lazy,' came a voice from behind us. My stepdad, Nanny.

'You're telling me,' I grinned.

Nanny smiled his big wide smile and gathered his salt-and-pepper dreadlocks into a ponytail, tying them with a length of string.

'Maybe we should run his raas round the park,' he said. 'Put together an exercise routine.'

'What — like a fitness regime for dogs?'

'Yeah, man.'

I shook my head. 'We'd never get him *to* the park in the first place,' I said.

Nanny grinned and then told me that he would catch me later. I watched him walk off down the road before dragging Zeus down the dark alleyway round the back of our house, past all the shit that the drug addicts and the working girls left behind – used condoms, needles, bits of clothing even. As we came up to our yard I looked down to the end of the alley, where it was blocked off by an empty house. A house where one of my crew, Ellie, had been held hostage a few months earlier over some trouble we had fallen into. I shook the memories from my mind and urged Zeus into the back yard.

The kitchen door was open and I could hear voices. My mum and her best friend Sue talking work. I untied Zeus and watched him pad slowly towards the house. Just by the drain he stopped and looked at something on the ground. He turned to me like he was asking for permission, and then back to whatever it was. Thinking that he was going to eat another snail and get sick again, I walked over and took a look. It was a silver earring. I smiled.

'Let me have that,' I told him, 'before you try and eat it, you fat git.'

I picked up the earring and took it inside, wondering which of the females in my life it belonged to.

It wasn't Della's. She was in the living room when I walked in, sitting on the sofa with her feet crossed underneath her, her toenails painted bright yellow. Her hair was braided and her legs were a polished caramel colour.

'Easy, Della.'

'Hey, Billy,' she replied, looking at me with her green cat's eyes. Something in those eyes told me she wasn't happy.

'What's up?' I asked.

'Nuttin',' she lied.

'Dell . . .'

'That stupid bwoi – that's what's up,' she said.

I had known Della since she was nine – in and out of care until she had been fostered by Sue. She was tough on the outside and soft as marshmallow within. And we knew each other like brother and sister. I could always tell when she was feeling down. The boy she was talking about was Jas, one of our crew and her boyfriend.

'What about him?' I asked.

'He stood me up – *again.*'

'Oh, right,' I replied, waiting for her to continue. Not that I knew Jas had stood her up ever before.

'Told me some shit 'bout he's got to see his cousin.'

'Which one?

'Dee,' she told me.

'Well maybe he had to see him – like he said?' I offered, hoping she wouldn't think that I was accusing her of over-reacting. Some chance.

'You sayin' I'm getting wound up for nuttin'?' she said, glaring at me.

'Nah, sister, none ah dat. Just that maybe he had some shit to sort out – is all.'

Della shook her head. 'Ain't the first time,' she said. 'He's been doing it on a regular basis – ever since he moved across town and that.'

Jas had moved to another part of the city after the trouble we'd had earlier that year. Not that he was ever at his mum's new place. Whenever I called he was out.

'I didn't know that,' I admitted.

'Like he's never got no time for me – not since I said I was goin' back to college.'

Della had started GCSE retakes at a local sixth form college to make up for failing them at school.

'Don't never reply to my texts, and when I see him, it's like his mind is somewhere else, you get me?' she continued.

'Nothing serious though?' I replied, hoping that they wouldn't fall out.

She must have read my mind. 'I'm ready to ditch that bwoi like a cold. Dust him off . . .'

'*But*—' I began.

'But *nuttin'*, Billy. Ever since I said I was goin' back to college he's been funny. Tellin' me that I'm wasting my time and saying that I'll get all stuck up and think that I'm better than him.'

I shrugged because I didn't know what to say. I'd had no idea they were arguing.

'And then when him want a little summat, man can't wait to come over – you know what I mean?'

'Yeah – too much info, Della,' I said, slightly embarrassed.

'*Fuck that!* What am I? I ain't bein' no stay-at-home, ready-when-yuh-ready woman.'

'I dunno what to tell you,' I said honestly. 'Sounds to me like you and him need to have a good talk—'

'What you think I been *trying* to do? He don't wanna know. Always out with his cousin or doin' this and that . . .'

I hadn't seen too much of Jas since the trouble about eight months earlier. I had got myself a part-time job and I'd only seen him now and then. Not that it was a problem. Jas was one of the gang and it didn't matter if I saw him or not. Man was always just a phone call away. That's what our little crew was like.

'Ain't taken me out nowhere – not even to the cinema. I have more nights out with you and Ellie.'

'You want me to talk to him for you?' I asked.

'Nah – I just want him to actually spend some time with me,' she told me.

'But he might listen to me,' I said.

'You shouldn't *have* to talk to him – he should *know* that I'm pissed off,' she replied.

'So what you gonna do?' I asked.

'Dunno . . . Like I said – I'm tempted to dust him off but I ain't sure that I can.'

I shrugged again.

'Put it this way,' said Della. 'Jas is treading on thin ice with me . . .'

TWO

Later that night I went to meet the other member of our crew, Will. I was supposed to be at work, filling shelves at a supermarket just out of the city centre, but I rang in sick. My supervisor told me that I had taken too much time off and warned me about my attendance.

I left the house and walked down to the main road that ran through the middle of our area, an inner-city collection of terraced streets and council blocks, high and low rise. At the first street corner I passed a gang of Somalian youths, hanging around and looking for something exciting to happen. Most of them had arrived in the last few years and they were still seen as outsiders by most of the other gangs. And there were plenty of those. Young crews, old crews. Male gangs, female gangs. Our streets were a place where you had to be in a crew, otherwise you'd get picked on, and I had learned from an early age that being part of a collective made things safer. That was how I had met and stayed close to my best mates.

Will grinned at me as I approached the end of his street, where he was standing talking to his brother, David. Will was my oldest friend: we had met at infant school and over the years he had grown bigger and bigger, helped by his addiction to weight training. Now, at sixteen, he was massive − 120 kilos of pure muscle, which he toned to perfection at the local gym four times a week.

'Easy, B,' he said.

'All right, Billy,' added David.

'What's up, man?' I asked.

David shrugged. 'Nuttin' − apart from I'm havin' another kid,' he said.

'Nah! That's how many now − five?' I said, shocked.

'Four,' Will corrected. 'Man's trying to start his own football team.'

David, who was as wide as his brother but shorter, smiled and shrugged again. 'Costing me dough in nappies,' he said.

'I ain't surprised,' I replied, laughing.

'Least they can all look after me when I'm old.'

'You is old enough now,' said Will.

David told us to stay out of trouble and went on to see their parents. Will shook his head.

'Like condoms don't exist, man,' he told me.

'Nuff presents Uncle Willy's gotta get at Christmas too,' I joked.

'Hey, skinny bwoi – nuh bother call me Willy.'

I grinned as he flexed the muscles in his arms to make his point.

'So what we doin'?' he asked. 'And ain't you supposed to be at work?'

'Rang in sick,' I told him.

'You knob – you're gonna get sacked.'

I shrugged. 'Like I give a fuck – job's boring and they don't pay me shit. I don't see why I should get paid less 'cos I ain't eighteen. I have to do the same amount of work,' I continued.

'It's the way of the world,' Will replied. 'Babylon mek the rules.'

'You sound like Nanny,' I told him. 'You turned Rasta?'

'Not yet,' he smiled.

We walked down towards the area around the community centre where there was a line of shops. A new kebab place had opened and the food was wicked. They sold all the usual stuff but they also did Greek salads and it was the only place where they gave you grilled haloumi cheese with every kebab. I loved the stuff and I was starving. As we reached the precinct I heard a shout go up and then a small kid came running past us, followed moments later by two older lads, one wearing a balaclava over his head. As the older lads passed Will stuck out his foot and the one in the hat tripped and landed flat on his front. He got up and swore. Will took a step towards him.

'What?' he asked.

The kid looked at Will, stepped back and then ran off. '*Grass!*' he shouted as he left.

'What'd you do that for?' I asked Will, wondering why he had bothered to get involved.

'Shouldn't be chasing little kids about,' he replied before changing the subject. 'You seen Jas?'

I thought back to my talk with Della, wondering whether I should tell Will. I decided that it wasn't my place to say anything. If Della had wanted him to know she would have told him herself.

'Nah,' I replied. 'How 'bout you?'

'Yesterday. I was working over by the Market Square, helping Jimmy with the re-wiring on some old place' – Will had recently started on an apprenticeship with an electrician Nanny knew and he was enjoying it – 'and Jas went by with a couple of older lads – Asian brothers.'

'Maybe he's setting up a bhangra group?' I joked.

'Dunno – he looked in a hurry. By the time I got out of the door to go say hello, man had gone.'

'He's been spending time with his cousins,' I told him.

Will shrugged. 'Now he's back on talkin' terms with his family I suppose he's gonna want to spend time with 'em,' he said.

It was true. Jas and his mum had been cut off by their relatives when Jas's mum left his dad. There was a huge scandal over it and Jas had always spoken about them like he hated them. His parents split when he was nine, and in the following seven years I hadn't seen him with any of them. And I knew that it had bothered him – having cousins he never saw. It was one of the reasons why the Crew meant so much to him. We were like family to him. Or we were.

I thought about my extended family, most of whom I saw at one-off occasions, and nodded my head. 'Must be that,' I agreed.

My family was all over the place. There was my mum's side, who were mostly Punjabi, and Nanny's family, who were either Jamaican English or a mix of different races. And then there was my biological dad Lynden and his family, who were all originally from Jamaica. Not that I saw my dad that often. It was Nanny who had brought me up and I saw him as my real father. Lynden was someone I had only recently met again, when the Crew was in trouble. It had started when we found

11

a bag of money belonging to some local drug dealer — an older youth called Busta. It had ended with the police, Nanny, Lynden and a gangster called Ronnie getting involved, not to mention a corrupt copper and a working girl, who wound up dead. But that was all in the past.

Will and I walked into the kebab shop and ordered — extra haloumi for me — before heading back to my mum's house. On the way I saw a couple of lads on mountain bikes, both Asian, doing street deals with white men in cars parked up at shaded kerbsides. I saw the working girls begin to congregate in their various pitches and watched as gangs of youths wandered the streets looking for action among discarded boxes, take-away containers and rusty beer cans. A police car sped past, its lights flashing, siren wailing. I heard shouts coming from open windows, screaming children. And every ten houses or so I could hear music blasting out of speakers: hip-hop, R&B, ragga and reggae. People in other parts of the city called our area 'the ghetto'. Sometimes it was easy to see why.

When we got back to mine Ellie was waiting for us. The youngest member of the crew, Ellie was still at school where she was doing her GCSEs. A couple of years earlier, I had stopped her from getting mugged by a couple of idiots, and we had been friends ever since. She was the baby of the gang and that's what we called her, especially when she got cheeky, which was all the time. She was wearing a baby-blue hooded top, jeans and trainers with baby-blue piping. Her blonde hair was piled on top of her head and her blue eyes were smiling along with her mouth.

'Where's my food, you horrible old men?' she asked, as she sat with her feet up on my bed.

'Make yourself at home,' I told her, putting the plates I had brought upstairs with me down on my desk.

'Well, your room is a pit anyway. My feet are cleaner than anything in *here*.'

'You want some of my kebab?' I asked, as Will took a plate and sat down next to her.

'Only if you got some of that rubbery cheese with it,' she said.

I grinned. Good job I'd ordered extra.

'I can't *believe* you went to the kebab shop without asking me too,' she continued as I unwrapped my food.

'Shut up, Ellie,' said Will.

'Della would *never* go without telling me,' she continued, totally ignoring Will.

I found a slice of grilled cheese and offered it to her. She took it and put the whole thing in her mouth, chewing it quickly. Then she jumped off my bed and grabbed my can of Pepsi from the desk, opened it and drank down half.

'*Eurgh!*' she said after she had finished her mouthful.

'I thought you liked it?' I said.

'*No* – I just wanted to see what it was like because you're always on about it. I just *had* to try it. It's horrible. It tastes like dishcloth!'

'Shame no one shoved one of *them* in your mouth,' said Will through a giant mouthful of chicken shish.

'Don't talk with food in your mouth, Willy,' replied Ellie. 'It's *very* rude and you'll get your bottom spanked.'

I raised an eyebrow.

'Oh, you dirty old man – I was only joking,' said Ellie.

'You wanna hang out for a bit?' I asked.

Ellie shook her head. 'No – just came over to say hello. What you doing tomorrow?' she asked.

'Nothing . . .' I said with a shrug.

'Good – you can take me to the pictures,' she told me.

'Er . . .' I began, only she didn't give me the chance to object.

She walked over to the door and opened it. 'See

you later, old man,' she said to me. Then she looked at Will.

'Bye, Willy,' she grinned.

The slice of cucumber that Will threw stuck to the back of the closed door for a second and then slid down to the floor. Ellie was long gone.

'That girl needs to get some manners,' said Will.

'Yeah,' I agreed.

'Cheeky likkle bloodclaat!'

THREE

The look on my mum's face the following evening told me that she was not in a good mood. Her forehead was creased and her dark brown eyes showed no sign of warmth. In front of her, on the kitchen table, was a pile of papers and files, stuff to do with work. But she wasn't looking at them. She was sitting staring into space, like she had seen a ghost. When I spoke to her I found out that it was more like a collection of ghosts, from her troubled past. Back when I was a little kid, she had had to work the street corners to feed me and put clothes on my back. Before Nanny had rescued us and made everything almost safe.

'They found a girl over on the other side of the ring road,' she told me – this was the concrete merry-go-round that separated the inner city estates from the city centre.

'A working girl?' I asked.

'Yes – over on the Whitelaw. Seventeen . . .'

I had learned from an early age to show the working girls respect and not to judge them for what they did. My mum worked with them now, offering counselling and advice on everything from drugs to childcare services, but back then, before Nanny, she had done exactly what they did and whenever she stopped to think about it she became sad.

'Was it a drug overdose?'

'No, Billy. She was killed by a punter, they reckon.'

'Who's *they*?' I asked stupidly.

'The police. They think she got into an argument with some bloke and he killed her. That's the third one in the past year.'

'Not including the girl that was killed when we got into that trouble?'

The girl, Claire, had been killed for letting us know where Ellie was being held. Her death had been the spark that led to the police getting involved in our troubles. Eventually the people behind the killing and the kidnappings were arrested and we returned to our normal lives.

'Not including her,' said my mum sadly.

'That's a lot of dead girls,' I said.

'Yes it is – the problem is that they are working

17

girls, not nice little college students, so their deaths don't warrant prime-time news—'

'But three over the past year—' I began.

'It happens all the time, Billy – it's not unusual. There are so many unsolved working girl murders in this country.'

'That's so fucked up.'

'Yes, it is, although I'd prefer it if you left that kind of language for your mates,' my mum replied.

'Yeah, yeah . . .'

'Anyway, the detective in charge of the case is Lucy Elliot – the one who helped us out over the summer.'

'*That's* a coincidence,' I said with a grin.

'Maybe. She checked the dead girl's background and apparently I sent her for drug counselling last year.'

I looked at the papers in front of her. My mum runs a women's drop-in centre and the papers were part of that.

'Is that why you're goin' through all those?' I asked.

'Yeah – she's coming over in a while and I've got to give her my notes, even though they're supposed to be totally confidential.'

'Is that legal?'

'The girl's dead, Billy. What does it matter

now?' She looked down at the papers and then away again, her dark eyes brooding and her beautiful face glum.

'You gonna be OK?' I said, concerned.

My mum shrugged. 'I always am,' she said quietly.

Nanny was sitting watching the local news when I walked into the living room. He had his hair down and there was a spliff between the fingers of his right hand that had burned itself out.

'Easy, my yout',' he said, not looking away from the telly.

'Summat interesting?'

'Dem arrest a whole heap of dealer dis mornin'.'

'Round here?' I asked, my interest picking up.

'All over the city – Operation Street Clean.'

I grinned. 'That's a stupid name.'

'Yeah, man – but it effective,' replied Nanny, stroking his beard before re-lighting his spliff.

'How many man they nicked?'

'Nuff – mostly for heroin,' Nanny told me. 'But dem even arrest some herb dealer man – like dem nah know dat de herb is not a drug.'

I sat down and watched the report with my stepdad. Nanny is a Rastafarian – not just one of them man that grows dreadlocks and pretends to be righteous; a proper Rasta. He doesn't drink alcohol or eat meat and he is the most relaxed and peace-loving man I've ever known. Not that he doesn't have a past. From what I've heard, before Nanny found his faith he was a bad man, but that was a long time ago. Now he tries to live as clean a life as he can, and he smokes weed as a religious sacrament. It brings him closer to Jah and helps free his mind of earthly, material thoughts. At least that's what he tells me. I've grown up around his faith, and even though I'm not a believer, the political side of it has affected the way I see the world. It's all about exposing the way the rich world exploits the poor and the lies we get told about history, where only white people ever did anything good and there was no real civilization before it was 'discovered' by the Greeks and Romans.

But he isn't racist or homophobic or any of the other stereotypes. He doesn't belong to a cult and he isn't a drug addict. Nanny is just Nanny, and if it hadn't been for him, my mum would have had a life twice as hard. He's been around since I was a kid and he is the person I turn to when I need advice and he's my real dad rather than my biological one. Like he's always said, *Any bwoi can mek a child but only a man tek care of him own*. I'm not even his and he treats me like I'm his blood. That's the kind of man he is.

'There's a lot of man gonna be upset by the raids,' I said, thinking about the drug gangs that came out in the early evening and provided sweets for those with an addiction to their particular brand of sugar.

'A whole heap a man,' agreed Nanny. 'Time tough fe dem man.'

'You know that copper's coming round in a bit?' I said, changing the subject.

'Yeah, man – Rita tell me.'

'You gonna hide that spliff?' I asked jokingly, wondering how Lucy Elliot would react.

'Nah – Babylon nuh like it, she can *bite* it,' grinned Nanny.

But instead of staying where he was he got up and left, telling me he had to go next door to Ellie's parents' house to fix a leak in their plumbing. Thinking about my mum and her mood, probably.

I was in my bedroom about an hour later when I heard a loud crack. The noise had come from outside and I ran downstairs to investigate. My mum and Elliot were at the front door, which was open. The door was wooden and there was a huge crack in one of the panels.

'What happened?' I asked.

'Dunno,' said my mum as she stepped out into the street.

'Hello, Billy,' said Elliot.

I looked into her brown eyes and smiled. She was quite fit for a copper, with shoulder-length blonde hair and a nice figure.

'Hi,' I replied, before following my mum out into the street.

Nanny and Ellie's dad, Brian, were already outside.

'What's goin' on?' I asked Nanny.

'Dunno. I was fixin' de plumbing when I heard a load of yout' shoutin' in de street. Nex' t'ing I hear that noise and come out here.'

'They've run off up the street,' added Brian, before turning to see Elliot.

'Hello, DI Elliot,' he said. 'That was quick.'

'She was visiting me,' explained my mum.

'Nothing wrong, I hope, Rita,' replied Brian.

'Just work,' said my mum.

'They were probably just messing around,' said Elliot, talking about the youths. She pointed across the street. 'They've knocked over a load of bins too.'

I knelt down and picked up a half brick that was lying in our small front yard.

'They must have thrown this,' I said, handing it to Elliot.

'Would you like me to get a patrol car sent round?' she asked my mum.

'Nuh bother wid dat,' replied Nanny. 'I can fix it quicker than dem man can reach.'

Elliot looked at Nanny like he was talking Martian and then asked my mum if that was what she wanted.

My mum shrugged. 'What you gonna do — arrest a load of twelve-year-olds?' she asked.

'No problem,' replied Elliot. 'Shall we finish up what we were doing?'

My mum nodded and led Elliot back inside as I watched. Ellie joined us on the street.

'What happened?' she asked.

'Just a load of kids pissing about,' I said.

I turned to go indoors but Ellie suddenly remembered that we had a date.

'What about the cinema, young man?' she asked, smiling.

'Oh yeah . . .'

'You don't *have* to take me,' she said, and for a minute I thought she was being serious and I would get out of it. But then she did an Ellie.

'You *could* just let me down and then I'd think that you don't love me any more. The shock of that would make me eat five huge pizzas every day and then I'd end up growing by two hundred kilos and in a year from now I'd

23

have to be dragged out of my bed by a *crane* and—'

'OK, OK,' I said. 'Take a breather, Baby. I'll take you but I ain't watching no stupid chick-flick about no romance.'

'That's fine with me,' grinned Ellie. 'We'll watch an *action* film with some big ugly bloke in it and the obligatory "tits out for the lads" bit – get some *real* culture.'

'Whatever. Let me get my money and my jacket,' I said to her.

'OK – I'll just go and make myself beautiful for you. Five minutes.'

She turned and went into her house as her dad and Nanny stood grinning.

'Yuh get turn inside out by that gal,' said Nanny.

'She's been doing that to me since she first began to talk,' added Brian.

'Just think what would happen if you was actually her boyfriend,' said Nanny.

'That's a headache I can do without, thanks,' I said.

Brian gave me a funny look. 'Are you saying that my beautiful daughter isn't good enough for you, young man?' His voice was stern.

'Er . . . I didn't mean anything by that, Mr—' I began, like an idiot.

Brian grinned. 'You're really going to have to be cleverer than that, son – if you want to compete with Ellie,' he told me.

'Very funny,' I said, as they both laughed at me.

PHONE CALL

'You do that thing?'

'Yeah, man, I done it exactly like you told me to do.'

'No comeback?'

'Nah – dem man trust me a'ready. I even got close to the man up top.'

'Don't mess it up, y'hear? Keep it cool.'

'So where's my likkle t'ing for sorting it?'

'Check my brother – he's holdin'.'

'Anyt'ing else you want me to do?'

'I'll let you know . . .'

FOUR

Two weeks later . . .

Della watched Jas as he wiped his nose and then blew hard into the tissue again.

'You got a cold or something?' she asked him.

'Yeah,' he told her.

'Best not give it me then – I got classes to attend.'

It was meant as a joke but the look on Jas's face told Della that he hadn't taken it that way.

'I was *kidding*,' she said, an attempt to smooth over the cracks that she could see in their relationship, not even a year old. Problems that seemed to be getting bigger every day.

'I gotta go in a minute,' said Jas.

'But you only got here half an hour ago.'

'Gotta go meet my cos up by the community centre – we're goin' out.'

'That Dee . . . ?' asked Della.

'Yeah?'

'You been spendin' a lot of time with him,' she went on.

'His old man has got a hosiery business – they make clothes and shit. I'm doin' some work for them.'

'What *kind* of work?'

'General running around.'

'Oh,' she said, looking out of her bedroom window.

Jas rolled over and got up from under the duvet, found his jeans and pulled them on.

'When you get a minute,' said Della, fighting back the urge to spit her words at him like they were venom, 'there's something I need to talk to you about.'

'What?' asked Jas.

'I thought you didn't have time now.'

'I ain't,' replied Jas.

'Well then, it can wait until you have.'

Jas creased his brow, looked at Della and then something in his head seemed to pop.

'*Suit yourself!*' he snapped at her.

'*Jas . . .*'

But he had already gone, slamming her bedroom door shut and stomping down the stairs. Della looked at the closed door for a moment and then she felt tears well up in her eyes. She stopped herself from crying and wiped the tears away. As she sat up, she wrapped her arms around herself and tried not to feel like she had just been used. But it didn't work. She wiped away more tears and then grabbed her mobile from the side table. She scrolled through her address book and found the number she was after.

FIVE

Ellie looked up at me and grinned. She was sitting on the floor.

'They're all minging,' she said.

I had asked her why she didn't have a boyfriend at school and she'd turned her nose up.

'They can't all be that bad,' I replied, shifting on my bed.

'They *are* – and anyway, I prefer older men.'

'What, like fifty-year-olds?' I said jokingly.

'Eurghh! I meant someone maybe a few years older than me – the lads at school are just immature.'

'Maybe if you give them a chance—'

'In their dreams,' she replied. 'This one lad, Jason, asked me out last week.'

'And?'

'*And* he didn't even bother to clean his teeth that morning. When he opened his mouth I counted three bits of food stuck in between them. *Yeah* – like I'm *really* gonna say *yes.*'

'*Nah!* That's *nasty*,' I told her.

'*Exactly* – why would I bother?'

I tried to think of a reason but couldn't come up with one. Instead I looked at my clock and saw that it was nearly eleven.

''Bout time you was heading home, young lady,' I told her.

Ellie groaned and called me an old man.

'You've got school tomorrow,' I reminded her.

'So? God – you're just like my dad sometimes—'

'Shut up.'

'Here I am telling you that I'm . . . er . . .' She stopped talking and went bright red.

'*What?*' I asked, wondering what she was on about.

'Nothing,' she said, smiling sweetly.

She stood up and adjusted her jeans, which were low-rise and showed off her underwear, a style that loads of girls had taken to wearing.

'Better get going,' she told me. 'I need my beauty sleep.'

'OK,' I said, walking straight into her trap.

'You *horrible* old man – you're *supposed* to say, "No you don't." You're *supposed* to tell me that I'm already beautiful *enough!*'

She had already left by the time I thought of a

way to dig myself out of the hole I had put myself in. I thought about going after her and apologizing but in the end I left it. She'd only smile and tell me she was having fun at my expense. She was funny like that. As I sat and thought about exactly how strange she was, my phone rang and Della's name flashed up on its tiny screen.

Della handed me a beer and then sat back down on the sofa in Sue's living room, folding her legs underneath herself.

'I said it wasn't goin' to happen again,' she told me for the fourth time since I had got there. 'Told myself that he wasn't goin' to get away with just comin' over for sex. But then I let it happen and now I feel like shit. *Again.*'

'What do you want me to say, Dell?' I asked her. 'I'm only going to tell you that you shouldn't have let it happen if you didn't want it to and you *know* that already.'

'I just wanted to talk to someone,' she replied. 'I know what I need to do.'

'So when are you going to tell him?'

She shrugged. 'He doesn't give me a chance. Always in a rush – doesn't answer his phone. He's working with his cousin now – did he tell you?'

'I ain't seen him for a while,' I told her.

'His uncle owns a factory or summat – Jas

said he's doing a bit of running around for him.'

'At least he's got himself a job — ain't like he's ever goin' to get back into school,' I replied.

Jas had been excluded from school for fighting in his final year and had never gone back.

'Yeah — I suppose,' said Della, although her voice told me that she didn't care about any job he might have found.

'The next time he comes round — tell him what's going on in your head. Don't let him think everything is cool,' I suggested.

'You know he flipped and stormed off earlier?' she said.

'Over what?' I asked.

'That's just it, Billy. It was over nothing. All I said was that I wanted to talk to him and he just snapped at me and then slammed the door behind him.'

I shrugged.

'But he has got a cold so maybe he's just not feeling too good,' she added.

'Dell, you're making excuses again. Look, I love him to bits — he's one of my oldest mates, but if he's out of order you gotta tell him,' I replied.

'But—' she began.

'But nothing, sis. You *have* to tell him.'

Della cuddled up against my shoulder before she replied.

'What if we fall out though – as friends? That's gonna mess up our whole crew and I don't want that.'

I played with one of her braids. 'Nothing will do that. We was all friends long before anything else happened and we can carry on—'

'No, it won't be the same, Billy. Don't pretend that it will, either,' she said.

'It might take a bit of time, but eventually he'll be the same old Jas – I promise.'

They say that you shouldn't make promises you can't keep. But what if you honestly believe that you *can* keep them and only find out later that you were wrong?

I woke up at around three in the morning, holding onto Della as we lay on the sofa. The TV was still on and there was some show on about lesbian circus performers. I untangled myself from Della without waking her and rubbed my eyes. Then, turning off the TV, I closed the living-room door behind me and let myself out.

Outside, the night air was fresh and chilly and I clapped my hands together as I walked home, trying to keep out the cold. Falling asleep in my clothes didn't help. I crossed the street and walked past a weary-looking working girl who asked me for a cigarette. I found my pack and offered it to her.

'Thanks,' she said, smiling at me. Two of her front teeth were missing and her hair looked like copper wire. And in her eyes I saw the lack of feeling that my mum's eyes showed whenever she remembered her past.

'No worries,' I replied, putting my fags away. I walked round onto the main road and then turned down the side street that ran parallel to Della's, two minutes from home.

Behind me I heard a screech of tyres and turned to see a black Fiat Punto pull up. Two youths wearing baseball caps got out. I held my position, wary but unafraid. I didn't know who they were and hadn't done anything to upset them so I wasn't worried. As they made to walk into a house, one of them nodded at me, letting me relax a little. They were just local rude boys — new to the area maybe. I nodded back and turned to walk on—

Then the lights went out as a pain like an electric shock sent down your spine hit me with its full force.

SIX

Ever since I was a little kid I'd heard stories about people being mugged or beaten up. The local paper carried news about daily street robberies. There were people all over our city who had been caught off guard by the kind of people who had beaten me up and robbed me of my possessions. But it had never happened to me before and as I lay in my bed the following morning, nursing my bruises, I felt ashamed and angry and helpless. I kept playing the mental images over and over in my head, like my own little movie, only in this version things were different: I hadn't ignored the youths. Instead I had realized what they were all about and run – not turned my back like some innocent fool. Or I had faced them down, beaten them up. Alternatives that acted as a defence mechanism against the feelings of embarrassment that welled up inside my chest.

No matter how many times I tried to change the ending in my head though, it didn't alter what had happened. I had woken up lying face down in the street, checked my pockets and found that they'd taken my mobile, my money and my mini-disc player. I had limped home but hadn't woken anyone up, and in the morning my mum had left for work by the time I went downstairs to the kitchen. Nanny, without making too much fuss, helped to clean me up a bit and put antiseptic lotion on my cuts. He sent me back upstairs again and rang work to let them know I wouldn't be coming in. Now he was sitting by my bed with a cup of green tea.

'Yuh know any of dem man from las' night?' he asked me as I took the cup from him.

'Nah – I ain't never seen them before.'

'Dem never say a word?'

I shook my head. 'I thought they was just some local rudies, Nanny. You know – some new faces an' that,' I told him.

'An' dem drive a black Fiat?' he continued.

'Yeah – all lowered, with alloys and spoilers.'

'You see whether dem Asian or black or what?'

I tried to picture them. I could see the caps on their heads and the sportswear but I couldn't really make out the faces.

'I can't remember.'

Nanny put his hand on my shoulder. 'Yuh get some res', my yout'.'

'Don't tell Mum, Nan.'

He gave me a quizzing look. I shrugged before replying.

'I don't want her gettin' stressed. She's got enough wrinkles – she don't need me adding no more. I got mugged. It happens . . .'

'Seen,' replied Nanny. 'But yuh can mek up yuh own story, bwoi. Me never lie to Rita before and me nah go start—'

'Just let me talk to her,' I said, before taking a sip. The tea was strong and bitter but the warmth of it made me feel better.

Not that I'd been too badly injured. I had a swollen lip, a cut under my eye and some bruising around my body. Nothing that I hadn't experienced before from fighting as a kid. The real injury was to my pride. I'd always had this idea in my head that I could walk around the roughest parts of the city and not get done over – because I knew the score. And I'd been wrong. Which hurt more than the bruises and the cuts.

'I'm gone,' said Nanny. 'The dinner nah go cook itself.'

'I'll be down in a bit,' I told him.

'Seen,' he replied, leaving the room and closing the door behind him gently.

Out of habit I reached over to the side table for my mobile but it wasn't there. The two lads had taken it. At first I winced as a pain shot through my side, but then I smiled to myself as I remembered Della losing her own phone a few months earlier. She was one of those people who kept all her numbers in the sim card memory and nowhere else. Like loads of others, she didn't have a clue what her best friends' numbers actually were. They just came up as names on her phone screen so she hadn't bothered to memorize them. Just like me. Luckily, I didn't have to go through all the hassle that Della had to. Maybe because I had too much time on my hands, or perhaps because I was organized, I had downloaded all my numbers onto my computer's hard disk.

I looked over at the dusty laptop and remembered Nanny's mate, Tek Life, getting it for me. He told me that he'd '*emancipate de bloodclaat t'ing*' from a friend in the education department and that's exactly what he had done. Nanny had joked that his name should have been Ronseal. I'd given him a hundred notes for it and the thing worked brilliantly. I got off the bed and went to my desk, left over from my time at school – not that I'd ever used it. I turned the laptop on and waited for the software to load so that I could pull Will's mobile number up. Once I'd written it down on a bit of paper, I headed downstairs again and rang him, hoping that he'd have his mobile on at work.

It was after seven when Will turned up at my house looking all pissed off and angry. He lowered his voice and whispered, 'Ain't you told yer mum yet?'

'Not yet – I've avoided her since she got in. She's out now anyway so you can stop with yer whispering nonsense.'

Will ignored my shit joke. 'You ring Jas?' he asked.

'Tried him – left a message. He ain't got back to me.'

'Does that bwoi ever answer his phone nowadays?'

I shook my head. 'Don't seem like it.'

I told Will that we'd give Jas until half-seven to show. After that we'd go on our own. Go to the house I saw the two youths entering the night before. Go and find out how tough they were when the numbers were even and the fighting face to face. I knew that there were other, more sensible ways to deal with the problem, like calling the police or leaving it alone, but that was the other man's way, not ours. Whether or not I liked it, we lived in streets where you had to protect your reputation. If you let a man give you a beating and steal your shit and said nothing to him, you were basically lost. Anybody's target. And I wasn't about to become one of those. At least that was the theory.

When Jas didn't show, I pulled on a hooded top and stepped outside with Will. I wondered where Jas was and for a moment I felt angry at him. We were supposed to be there for each other all the time but that was obviously changing.

We passed Ellie's mum in her small front yard, weeding and digging her flowerbed, as we set off. She said hello and asked me if I was going to see Ellie later. 'She's upset about something at school,' she told me. 'I thought you could talk to her, Billy. She listens to you.'

'We're just goin' to sort something out,' I replied. 'Won't take too long. I'll pop round when I get back or I'll call her tomorrow, Mrs S.'

'Thank you, Billy,' she replied.

If she had known what we were about to do, I'm sure Ellie's mum wouldn't have given me the look that she did. One that said, 'Aren't you lovely!' I decided that Ellie was probably having a strop about a boy or something and made a note to check on her later. Then I followed Will down the street, ready to find out why the youths from the night before thought that they could mash me up and get away with it.

* * *

The door was answered by a blonde woman – she was maybe eighteen or nineteen. She was wearing flared jeans and a small red top with yellow flowers printed on it. Her hair was tied up in a bun on the top of her head. She was fine.

'Can I help you?' she said, smiling.

'Er—' I began but Will cut me off.

'We're looking for two man that live here.'

The woman looked confused. 'There aren't any men that live here,' she replied.

'Nuh bother lie!' barked Will.

The woman stepped back a bit and then her eyes filled with anger. 'Who the hell do you think you are? *Fuck off!*'

I held up my hand to try and calm her down. 'Look, I'm sorry, but I was beaten up outside your house last night.'

The woman looked from me to Will and then she kind of half smiled, only her eyes were still angry. 'And that's my business *because* . . . ?' she asked.

'The people that did it pretended to walk into your house,' I told her, realizing straight away that I was being a dickhead. Why would they show me where they lived and then mug me?

'Well they don't live here,' she replied, her eyes calming.

'Drove a black Fiat – lowered – body kit,' I added.

She thought for a minute. 'There's loads of cars like that around here – it's like a race track sometimes,' she replied. 'But I don't know anyone that drives one of them.'

'Oh,' I said, as Will gave me a look that said, 'Let's go.'

'Sorry,' said the woman.

Behind her I heard another woman's voice asking who was at the door and then a baby began to cry.

'Better get back to the girls,' said the woman.

'Er, yeah,' I said, as she shut the door in our faces.

'So much for that then,' Will added.

I looked at him, shook my head and walked off, in the direction of the community centre. He stood and watched the door for a bit. Then he came after me.

SEVEN

The precinct around the community centre was buzzing with people as we got there. Gangs of kids milled about, drinking from green plastic bottles of cider and fortified wine, smoking spliffs and cigarettes. They stood around in groups. One of these was fifteen strong, with an older lad circling on his mountain bike, a cap pulled down on his head and big headphones around his neck. From across the main road a yellow light filtered up into the darkness from the mosque that stood proudly at the centre of the street, its twin minarets towering into the sky. A police car sidled by, its occupants looking bored, and then a gleaming black BMW, windows smoked out and sound system blasting bass-heavy tunes. Somewhere in the distance there was a siren blaring.

As we walked down the steps into the area by the shops, the older lad stopped his bike and watched us, his eyes never leaving our faces. Will nodded at him, recognizing him from around, and we walked past the shop fronts without making too much fuss. As we passed the biggest group I heard a snigger and then someone coughed loudly. I turned to see three youths, about fourteen but thinking bigger, staring at me.

'Wha'?' I asked them.

Instead of replying they just looked at each other and then grinned to themselves, like I was the butt of some joke that I hadn't heard. Maybe it was the mugging or maybe I was just in a bad mood but the look on the face of one of the lads riled me so much that I grabbed him around the throat and threw him into some railings. As his friends made to move, the older lad pulled up and got off his bike.

'*What you doin', man?*' he demanded.

I looked at him and then at the lad on the floor. 'What's it to yer?' I asked, as Will let out a sigh and stepped up.

'You got a problem – deal wid it. Don't tek it out on dem yout's,' said the older lad.

'He didn't mean it,' replied Will.

I turned and gave him a look but he just shrugged.

'We's out lookin' for someone,' he explained. 'Yer man there should watch his mout'.'

The older lad looked at Will as though he was a circus freak and then turned back to me. 'Anytime yuh want mess wit' me . . .' he said.

Something in my head snapped as he spoke and I lunged at him, only to feel myself being plucked from the ground like I weighed the same as a balloon. Will dragged me away as the younger kids started to laugh.

'Yuh better run to the police, *batty* bwoi!' shouted someone.

'*Leave it!*' shouted Will, looking into my eyes.

'I ain't leavin' *shit*!'

'They're kids, man — foolish street rats. Same as we was at that age. We got summat else to get on with.'

'But—' I began.

'But nuttin', Billy. Let's go check out the community centre. And if dem man is still here when we pass back this way — I'll *help* you do 'em,' he growled.

The anger in my head subsided and I was my usual self again, embarrassed at the way I had reacted to a bunch of idiots. I made a mental note to remember the older lad, however, just in case I bumped into him on the street somewhere else.

There was a load of fencing around the old library that stood empty next door to the community centre. A gap had been left where the steps up to the centre were and we walked through it. The library was being refurbished, and was due to re-open in a year – not that many of the youths in the area ever used it for anything other than stealing the CDs. For some reason I had a flashback to when I was eight, holding Nanny's hand as he led me into the children's book section and sat with me as I read from the pages of books that always seemed to be about the same things. The kids in them lived in country villages or visited family in big old houses and there was never anything in their lives that they had to worry about. They got into scrapes with smugglers and villains but things were always fine by the end.

I remembered that I'd asked Nanny why there were no police cars or working girls in the books. Where was all the rubbish on the streets and the homeless people? I remembered comparing the stories I read to my own life and finding nothing in them that spoke to me about what things were really like. That was why I'd stopped reading by the time I went to secondary school, and only started again when my mum lent me a crime novel by James Lee Burke. Not that he wrote about my life either. Just different lives, ones that weren't full of old language and posh kids on boating lakes, or fantastical worlds full of inter-changeable goblins and wizards.

I only snapped out of my thoughts when Gary, one of the community workers, said hello to me.

'You off yer head or something?' he asked, with a grin.

'*What?*' I asked.

'I said hello about four times before you heard,' he told me.

Will told him about the mugging and then asked him if he had seen a car like the Punto around recently.

Gary shrugged. 'There's a few of them around,' he said. 'I saw a red one the other day – Fiat Punto with all the stupid sports stuff on it—'

'The one we're looking for is black,' I told him.

'Dunno,' he said, shrugging again.

We stood and chatted for a while, watching the kids playing table tennis and shooting pool on old tables with ripped cloth. The same tables me and Will had played on when we were younger. At the far end of the main hall was a stage that was used now and then by local bands and the odd reggae sound system. Recently there had been a series of garage events staged too, until about a month ago when someone had been stabbed to death in the precinct after a gig – with a bottle of Moët. That had put a stop to the garage nights for good.

'Seen your mate Jas the other day,' Gary told us.

'Oh yeah?' said Will. 'I ain't seen that bwoi for a while.'

Gary gave us both a funny look. 'Dunno if I should say, but . . .' he began, only to stop.

'But *what*?' I asked, as I heard rain begin to pound the community centre roof.

'He was outside, standin' next to a phat car with two other Asian lads – older ones.'

'That'll be his cousins,' I told him.

'Oh right . . . it's just that those older lads are takin' over from Busta and his crew—'

'*What?*' I looked at Will in surprise.

'Well, since all that shit with you and Busta, and him goin' inside, the dealers have changed a bit,' continued Gary. 'There's a load of whispers goin' round that a gang of Asian lads have set up—'

'The lads that Jas was with?' asked Will.

Gary looked unsure for a minute. 'I don't wanna get no one in no—'

'We ain't gonna *tell* no one,' I said. 'What d'you think we are – *grasses*?'

Gary looked away and then back at me, as the rain on the roof began to sound like hail. 'A load of dealers have been getting sent down – there's people talking.'

'Yeah I seen that on the telly,' said Will. 'Operation *Batty Clean* or some other fool-fool t'ing.'

'Well, the lads that Jas was with – they're part of this new gang, although if anyone asks, I never told you shit.'

'Don't worry,' said Will.

'It's just that if he's hanging around with dealers and they get arrested, Jas might . . .'

I looked at Gary in shock. 'Are you telling us that Jas is *dealing*?' I asked, convinced that he was going to say that I had misunderstood him. He didn't.

'Some of the younger kids were talking the other day . . .' He came to a stop, then tried to change the subject by asking whether we would help him with the Sunday league football team.

'Hold on. Just tell us about Jas,' I insisted.

But Gary said that he had to go and walked off, leaving me and Will standing in a kind of shock. Jas was the most anti-drugs person I knew – well into kick boxing and all kinds of other sport. He even had a pop at me when I smoked a bit of weed. There was no way he was dealing, although that didn't mean that his cousins weren't. And if he got a reputation from hanging with them, people would assume he was dealing anyway, regardless of the facts. As we walked back to mine in the pouring rain, past a now-deserted precinct, I told Will that we would have to get hold of our friend as soon as we could.

'We need to get out of this bloodclaat rain first,' he growled, as a police car sped by, sirens wailing and lights flashing.

I nodded, then remembered that we had originally set out to look for the lads who had mugged me. Only they were about to become the least of my worries. *Time tough*, Nanny had said about the dealers arrested in Operation Street Clean. He could just as easily have been talking about us. Time was about to get hard, like Admiral Tibet sang in a reggae tune Nanny played now and then. It was a serious time.

EIGHT

Jas watched his cousin Dee pull to a stop at the kerb. He left the engine of his black Honda Accord running and got out.

'Easy, Cos.'

'Yes, Dee – what a *gwan*?' asked Jas, eyeing the new car with envy.

'Nuttin', you know,' replied Dee. 'You like the wheels?'

Jas nodded. 'It *yours*?' he asked.

Dee smiled and shook his head. 'Hired it – no point spendin' big dollars on a car when you can borrow one.'

'It's *rude*, man,' replied Jas, his head beginning to feel light.

'Come, let's go check Kully and the rest of them man.'

Jas thought about his last meal the evening before. He looked at the clock on his mobile. It was gone midday. Just as he looked at the time his stomach grumbled. In his head the whisper started.

'Can we get some food first?' he asked.

Dee checked his own mobile and said yes. He hadn't eaten for a while himself and was feeling hungry. 'Let's go down that Boyds up Clarendon Park,' he said.

'Is that a good place?' asked Jas, unsure of where Dee meant.

'Yeah, man – biggest fry-ups in town, bro. Full English,' smiled Dee.

They got into the car and Dee pulled away, narrowly avoiding a youth riding his bike erratically.

'Stupid dickhead!' shouted Dee, over the booming hip-hop CD. Unsurprisingly the youth on the bike didn't hear him and rode off down the street.

'Knob,' added Dee, before filling Jas in on what they had to do later.

Jas nodded. He was beginning to get an ache behind his eyes and a longing in his brain. The whisper again, like a beautiful woman talking softly into his ear, urging him. His stomach turned twice. It was a sensation he was getting used to.

The food just made Jas feel worse. Twice he had to hurry to the loo as a vice-like grip made his stomach shrink around the greasy food he was shovelling into it. When he returned the second time his cousin asked him if he was OK.

'Just got the runs a bit,' replied Jas, rubbing his belly.

Dee grinned. 'Nuh worry yuhself, Cos – we all get,' he told him with a wink.

'Nah – it ain't cause of that t'ing deh. I'm just feelin' queasy,' countered Jas.

'Whatever you say, rude bwoi,' replied Dee with a sniff.

'Me mum put too many chillies in that curry last night – I ain't had one for a while,' added Jas.

'Man, I can't even look at that shit no more – it's like pourin' drain cleaner in yer belly.'

Jas looked at his cousin and tried to grin, only his stomach twisted and turned for a third time and he ran to the toilets. Only after he'd returned did his stomach begin to calm down, and eventually begin to grumble again. He looked at his breakfast for a minute and then began to wolf it down. By the time his plate was clean, his cousin was impatient to get going.

'Come – it's nearly half one. I told Kully we'd be there at one,' said Dee.

As if to emphasize this, his phone started to make music. He answered it and lowered his voice. It was his brother Kully.

'I said one p.m. – I'll be there in a minute . . .'

Jas listened to Kully talking on the other end of the phone, unable to make out what he was saying.

'I got Jas wit' me, bro,' continued Dee.

Jas couldn't hear what Kully replied to that but then Dee told him everything was cool and rang off.

'Come,' he said to Jas, rising from his chair. 'Let me pay for this and we'll get goin'.'

'You want some dough?' asked Jas, reaching for his pocket.

Dee shook his head. 'Don't be stupid. I don't tek money from me own blood.'

'But—' began Jas.

'But nuttin – it's just wicked to have you around again, bro,' Dee told him.

Jas felt a tingle reach his neck from the base of his spine and he smiled.

'Ain't no Punjabi word for "cousin",' Dee told him. 'Just brother.'

They met Kully outside a row of lock-up garages on an estate at the opposite end of the city. He looked angry about something.

'What up, bro?' asked Dee.

Jas stood at his side, waiting for his older cousin to reply.

'Too much informer – *that's* what up. A whole lot of nex' man just been taken down.'

'You what?' replied Dee, looking shocked.

'Ten man from two different estates,' continued Kully. 'We need to get things tight.'

Dee nodded. 'So we'll close everything down. My man here is ready to do the go-between t'ing anyhow,' he said, gesturing to Jas.

Kully smiled and gave Jas a hug. 'Little bro – how yer doin'?' he said.

'Cool,' replied Jas, feeling the same tingle.

He remembered what Kully had said to him when they had first got back in touch. The warm feeling it had given him. He had waited for so long to be accepted again and now he felt like he was really part of something. Part of his family again. He played the conversation over in his mind:

'You know – even after what happened wit' yer old man – we never stopped thinking about yer,' Kully had said.

'Me an' all,' said Jas.

'Ain't right for us to have family we don't know – you get me?'

Jas thought about the years he'd been apart from his family. He remembered asking his mum over and over again about his cousins. Especially Kully, who he'd looked up to as a child. He grinned.

'So we just gonna stand here or we gonna do summat?' he asked.

'True say,' agreed Dee. 'Now let's get to business.'

Kully undid a padlock and started to raise the door to one of the lock-ups.

'This is easy, Jas, don't worry. Just remember to keep yer mouth shut tight, OK?'

'OK,' said Jas, feeling his stomach go off again.

'There's man chatting people business all over town — I ain't getting hooked up 'cos of no informer.'

'No problem, Kully,' replied Jas.

Kully smiled as they ducked under the door and then let it fall back down. He turned on a light.

'And when I catch dem man — believe me, someone ago get burned,' he said.

Jas thought about Billy and Della for a moment, knowing what they would say if they knew what he was doing. But then he remembered what Dee had said to him a few months back. All that kids stuff was finished with. Crews and shit. It was time to stand up on his own two feet and get a slice of the pie. Take his place where he belonged — with his own flesh and blood. *Apna khoon*. Time to take what was his. If he didn't, somebody else would. And he wasn't about to give up his crust for *no* man.

After they had finished at the lock-up, Kully left them to drive back to the community centre, where Dee parked up in a side street and started to make phone calls. Within ten minutes a lad wearing a cap with a hooded top pulled over it turned up and got in the back seat, handing over envelopes stuffed with cash.

'Everyt'ing cool?' asked Dee.

'Yeah, man – sweet,' said a voice that sounded familiar to Jas.

He turned to see Divy Kooner grinning back at him.

'What up, Jas?' asked Divy.

'A'right,' replied Jas, wondering what Divy was doing in Dee's car.

Dee noticed the tension between the two of them and asked what was going on.

'Nuttin',' lied Jas.

'We used to have a t'ing, goin' back a while,' replied Divy. 'Yer man there gave me a few beatings when we was kids.'

'An' you needed all a dem,' snapped Jas.

Dee laughed. 'Cool yuh temper, bro,' he said to Jas, before turning to Divy.

'What?' asked Divy, shrugging. 'I ain't saying shit to him.'

'Just leave it – Jas here is my family, you get me?'

Divy looked shocked.

'And I don't care what happened with you two in the past – Jas is my connection with you from now on – clear?'

Divy looked at Jas and shrugged again. 'Yeah – whatever,' he replied, before speaking to Jas. 'So how's yer likkle crew, rude bwoi?'

'I ain't doin' that no more – you get me?'

'So you ain't knockin' round with that half-breed mofo Billy?'

Jas fought an urge to smash Divy's flat nose even further into his face. Instead he remembered Dee's instructions. *Nothing gets personal. Just do the exchange and gone.*

'No, I don't hang wit' dem man no more,' replied Jas.

Dee grinned and pulled out a wrap of cocaine. He took a CD cover from his glove box and got out a plastic loyalty card from some supermarket.

'Seein' as we's all kissed and made up,' he told them, 'we may as well lick da peace pipe.'

Jas looked at Divy and shrugged. The pain behind his eyes was still there and he was ready for it to disappear. The whisper that echoed softly around his head returned and told him that it was OK. *It was OK . . .*

'Looks like you an' me might just have summat in common,' laughed Divy, as Dee handed him the CD cover and a small silver pipe.

PHONE CALL

'What's that noise in the background, bro? Sounds like man crying.'

'It is.'

'Nah – you're takin' the piss.'

'I'm serious. Some young bwoi who can't handle the time – plenty of dem man in yah. Anyway I never called you to chat 'bout no pussy bwoi.'

'I got it covered, rude bwoi – nuh worry 'bout dat.'

'I ain't worried, Divy. You mess things up and is you gonna be doin' the worryin' – hear me?'

'Yeah – don't get funny 'bout it.'

'So you ready?'

'Yeah – I done it already. This morning—'

'Who?'

'A few more of the young ones.'

'Nice – hold it down after this one though. We'll leave it a few weeks and then go for one of the others.'

'One of them man up top?'

'Exactly. Till then get started on them other things I told you.'

'No problem – I got that all sorted. They ain't gonna know what hit 'em, man.'

'Seen. Just remember to watch yer back, bwoi. You is no good to me in no police cell.'

'Sack that – ain't happenin'.'

'Anyt'ing else?'

'Yeah, actually there is. It's about that Jas . . .'

NINE

I didn't bother to call Ellie the next day even though I'd told her mum that I would. My thoughts were taken up by the whispers surrounding Jas, and I was trying to think of a way to get hold of him. Not at his mum's new house — it was like he didn't even live there. He wasn't answering his phone and the last time he had replied to a text message of mine had been about a month earlier. It was all I thought about during my early shift at the supermarket. One of the only good things about my 'job' was that it involved no thought at all. I just grabbed boxes from a wheeled cage and opened them before stacking the contents on the correct shelf. Nothing to it. It gave me enough time to work through the things I had going on in my head — which was loads, most of the time.

After work I decided to catch the bus into the city centre and I wandered around for a bit, with nowhere to go and nothing to do. I looked in a few shop windows and watched people go by, but all the time I was thinking about Jas. The problem with whispers in our area was that once they started to grow, people changed the facts and eventually things got way out of hand. It had happened to a bloke a few years earlier, a postman who was wrongly rumoured to have been linked to child abuse. I was too young to know where the rumour had begun but eventually the entire community heard it. Kids would throw stuff at his windows – eggs and flour and things and he was beaten up a few times. Then he just disappeared.

Two months later his body was found floating in a canal out in the country somewhere and the press jumped on the story. It turned out that he had once written poetry for children and worked with them. That was all. But someone had changed the story for whatever reason, and the man had ended up dead. No one had bothered with the facts or tried to ask him about it all. It just became an accepted truth that he had abused kids. The rumours around Jas weren't that serious but once they got out of hand, who knew what would happen?

But I had to get in touch with him to let him know – warn him even. I could see why he was spending so much time with his family. I reckon I would have been the same. As we were growing up Jas had often talked about his relations and how he felt isolated from them. I understood that being back with them was a big deal for him and that he needed his space to deal with it all. I just wanted to tell him that I was still his friend, regardless, and that he meant as much to me now as he ever had done. Nothing was going to change the fact that we were friends. Nothing.

After I had walked around for about two hours I found myself standing in front of a bar where my dad ran the door staff. It was a weekday afternoon and there weren't any doormen on but I could see my dad standing at the bar talking to a woman. He was wearing a long black leather jacket and I could see that he had his hair in corn-row braids – different from the last time I'd seen him. Part of me wanted to walk on by but I didn't. Instead I opened the door and walked in. The barman looked me up and down. He began to shake his head and said something to my dad, who turned round. He grinned and told the barman that I was OK.

'Yes, Billy!' he said, grabbing me around the shoulders and then pulling me into a hug.

I pulled away after a moment and looked at him.

'Hey, Lynden,' I replied.

'*Wha*'? Check my yout', man!'

The woman he had been talking to smiled and said hello as my dad carried on.

'Him nuh even call me Dad.'

I was tempted to walk straight out again. Dads stay around when you're born and look after you and shit. They teach you to swim and ride a bike and take you down the park. Lynden hadn't done any of that for me, so why would I call him Dad? I was about to say something but then I stopped myself. Living in the past is no way of dealing with the present, and besides, I needed to ask him some stuff.

'So what can I do fe yuh?' he asked me, ruffling my hair like I was five years old again.

I shrugged. 'Just wanted to have a chat,' I told him. 'I was walking by and I seen you was in here so I thought—'

'That you'd come check for your old man,' he said, finishing my sentence in a way that pleased him but wasn't the truth.

'Summat like that,' I told him.

'Seen . . .'

He nodded his head for a while and then told the woman that he would call her later. She smiled at him and said she had to go get her hair done anyway. Lynden watched her leave.

'A one *fine* woman, dat,' he said with a grin.

'Yeah?' I asked.

'Fe true, my yout'.'

He told me to go and take a seat in one of the booths that lined the wall opposite the bar and ordered some drinks. Then he came over and sat down with me.

'So,' he said, smiling again, 'what brings you to see me?'

A little while later he took me to another of the bars that his door firm ran and got me some food. I wasn't complaining. It was getting colder outside and I needed to warm up and at least now my mouth was hot. It was the jerk chicken with rice and a really spicy sauce that made me think of Nanny's hot pepper curries – guaranteed to clean out your system. It felt like my blood was on fire and by the time I'd finished I had gone through about eight bottles of water. My dad just laughed at me as he dropped piri-piri sauce on his plate to make his food even hotter. Man had to have a stomach made of cast iron.

One of the bar staff cleared our stuff away and my dad pulled a short spliff from his pocket and lit it. I pulled out my fags, all five of them, and lit up too.

'Dem t'ing gwan mash yuh up, Billy,' he said to me, as he took a long, hard draw on his herbs.

'What — and that shit ain't?' I replied.

'Herb, man. Healing of we nation,' he said, sounding like Nanny.

'Ain't you gonna get stress for smokin' in here anyways?' I added.

My dad looked around and then back at me. He winked. 'Who's gonna mek me stop, kid?'

He was involved in lots of stuff, my dad, most of it on the wrong side of what most people call conventional. And I didn't have to question what he'd just said. There were probably only a handful of people in the city who could make my dad do anything he didn't want to. And they were his mates. Not that I thought his *bad bwoi business* was cool or anything. What he did was up to him. What I needed from him was a bit of information. And if he wanted to act the hard man while he gave it to me — so be it.

As he stubbed out his spliff I asked him what was on my mind.

'You and Ronnie got anyone doing shit in the neighbourhood?'

My dad gave me a funny look and then grinned. 'You want me fe inform pon mi own crew?' he said jokingly.

'Don't be stupid . . . Dad.'

He grinned even wider at that and I explained about what Gary had told me and Will. He listened intently and then looked around some more.

'Come, Billy – let's go to my car. Too many man run up dem mouth nowadays – we need some privacy.'

We walked out of the bar and ended up sitting in his black Saab turbo. He built a fresh spliff for himself as he spoke.

'Every time a man get arrested, there's always new people ready to step up. Drugs is big business – you know that.'

'So, these Asian lads – they *are* takin' over?'

My dad shook his head. 'They might be one of a few smaller gangs doin' shit but the overall t'ing ain't run by no one.'

That surprised me. My dad's business partner, Ronnie Maddix, had told us that he wanted to take over everything after our trouble with Busta. Ronnie had helped us out – saved our lives probably – but I didn't believe that he wasn't filling in where Busta and his boss, a corrupt police detective called Ratnett, had left off. There was just too much money to be made.

'What about Ronnie?' I asked, knowing that my chances of getting a straight answer were about a minus ten.

My dad exhaled a steady stream of smoke and then shook his head. 'Ronnie ain't got nothing to do with it – he wants to go legit.'

'*Fuck off*,' I said, surprised and feeling like he was trying to take me for a ride.

'A who teach yuh to swear so?' he asked me, grinning again. 'Not yuh mother—'

'Leave her out of it,' I replied. My voice must have been stern because my dad cocked an eyebrow and then let it go.

'I'll see what I can find out for yer,' he said.

'I don't care who's doin' what – I just wanna know if Jas is part of it, that's all,' I told him.

'Whatever – just mind yuh motion. Plenty man getting nicked all over town, Billy. If I didn't know yer and I heard you asking all these questions – I'd think you was a grass.'

'You don't, do you?' I asked, worried for a moment. It wasn't even that I was *that* concerned about the dealers. I couldn't have cared less. They knew the risks before they started. I just didn't want my dad to think that I was a grass. Not my dad.

'Nah – I know you better than you think. Just mind who you ask questions. All it takes is one whisper in a man ear and the next thing you know, you got yourself a rep.'

I didn't know it then but by the time my dad had dropped me off outside my mum's house, things had already spun way out of our control. The whispers were about to become shouts . . .

TEN

Ellie was waiting for me when I got in. She was petting Zeus, even though she liked to tell people that she hated animals. Once, when she was about six, her parents had taken her to a zoo and she had been messing about, sticking her fingers into the monkey cage. She had peeled a banana and offered it to one of the monkeys, and just as he grabbed for it, she pulled it away, stuck her tongue out and took a big bite. The monkey got its own back by reaching out of the cage and scratching her leg. She had never forgotten it. As I walked into the living room, she pushed Zeus away and pretended she had been watching the telly.

'See?' I said to her. 'And you tell me you don't like him.'

'I wasn't anywhere near him,' she lied. 'He's got bad breath and a smelly bum – why would I touch him?'

Zeus stood in front of her, wondering why she had stopped playing with him. He turned his giant head towards me and then padded over. I crouched and gave him a few pats on the back of his head.

'Don't worry, Zeus,' I whispered to him. 'She loves you really.'

I was expecting Ellie to get on one and tell me that she didn't love the big fat smelly thing but she surprised me. She turned to look at me and her face was full of sadness. Something had really upset her. I let Zeus out of the living room and closed the door behind him.

'What's up?' I asked her, as her eyes began to water.

'You said you'd come and see me yesterday,' she told me.

I walked over and sat down next to her, putting my arm around her.

'I was busy, and anyway that's not the reason you're crying – it's something else,' I said to her.

'I'm not crying,' she said, through tears.

I pulled her closer and gave her a hug. 'Someone been mean to you?' I asked, wondering what was up.

She nodded and then buried her head in my shoulder.

'Ellie, I can't hear you if you do that. Tell me what happened.'

She mumbled something and then pulled her head away. I took a tissue from my pocket and gave it to her.

'You've snotted all over my top,' I said with a grin.

'No I haven't,' she said, wiping her nose. 'It was already there.'

'Ellie . . .'

'They're picking on me and I don't like it,' she told me.

'Who's picking on you – someone at school?'

She nodded. 'They keep calling me names and writing stuff all over the place.'

'Who?'

'The older boys – and some of the girls too. It's not the same since Della went. I hate it,' she added.

I could feel myself getting angry. No one picked on Ellie. Not if they wanted to keep their teeth.

'You got names for these lads?' I asked sternly.

She nodded quietly, wiping away more snot from her face before doing the same thing to my top.

'Leave that,' I told her. 'Just tell me who they are.'

'That's just it – I can't. If I tell you who they are then they'll know and everything they've been saying about me will be true and then I'll be in even bigger shit and—'

'Take a breath, Baby,' I told her.

'But . . .' she began again.

'Forget about what they'll do – just tell me who they are, will you? And why they're doing it.'

Later that evening, after Ellie and me had eaten a curry that Nanny had made, I called Della and Will, and left another message for Jas. Will brought Della with him and we moved upstairs to my bed-room, where I put on a Buju Banton CD. As usual, Jas didn't even bother to reply. The rest of us took our usual positions in my bedroom, with Della and Ellie lounging on my bed, me on the floor next to it and Will sitting on my swivel chair.

'Bwoi – dis CD old, man,' grinned Will.

'Still wicked though,' I replied, not smiling back.

Will picked up on my mood and asked me why I had called the Crew together.

'A load of lads have been picking on Ellie,' I told him.

'You what?' asked Della, her eyes blazing and her shiny, chocolate-brown shoulders tense, corded with muscle.

'At school,' added Ellie.

'*Who?*' Della demanded. 'An' why we sittin' here? Mek we go find dem bwoi and bus' dem mouth shut—'

'It's not that simple,' I said.

'Oh yeah – it is *that* simple,' argued Della, tensing up even more.

I looked at Will, who was now just listening.

'They're calling her a grass – all of us, actually.'

'Huh?' said a shocked Della.

'They're calling Ellie all kinds of names and slagging us all off too. Including Nanny.'

'But—' she began, only for Will to cut in.

'And it ain't just kids messing about?' he asked Ellie.

She shook her head before replying. 'No – they keep on doing it and there's some graffiti on a wall down by the school about Nanny too.'

'Shit . . .' said Della.

'Exactly,' I agreed.

'It's still kids pissin' about,' countered Will. 'We ain't no grasses . . .'

'The lads at school said that we'd grassed up one person and we could do it again,' Ellie told us.

'What – *Busta*?' asked Della. 'But that bwoi is a nonce and anyway we didn't grass.'

It was Busta who'd had Ellie kidnapped. Busta who'd helped to get a young girl called Claire killed. He *was* a nonce, and the way I saw it, it had been our duty to give him up. Not that we actually grassed on him anyway. It was Nanny and two of his mates who had made him see the error of his ways. Getting caught was his own fault.

'It's just stupid kids – I told you,' repeated Will. 'No big deal—'

'Apart from the fact that Ellie is getting shit,' I reminded him.

'And people are writing stuff on walls,' added Della.

'Well that's easy,' I said. 'Let's go and get rid of it.'

'How?' asked Della.

'There's some old paint in the shed in the yard. We'll go and paint over it,' I said.

'But what about the people who are picking on me?' asked Ellie, looking concerned.

'Let's go do this and then we'll sort that out tomorrow,' I told her. 'I'm working until twelve but then I'll come over to the school.'

She smiled at me before replying. 'OK then – but I don't want to come with you tonight. I've got . . . homework to do,' she said.

I was going to tease her about being scared but I caught myself just in time. Ellie was sensitive at the best of times. Instead I got up, leaned over and gave her a kiss.

'*Woooo!*' laughed Della, as Ellie went red.

'What?' I asked, confused.

'She'll be dreaming *good* tonight,' teased Della.

'*Shut up*, you old woman!' replied Ellie, looking at me and then away.

'Women, man,' I said, 'I bet *they* don't even know what they're on about.'

'Too right, bro,' agreed Will. 'Weirdos.'

'Ah poor Willy – no one to kiss him – does Willy want a *kissy*?' teased Della.

'I'll give you summat in a minute,' said Will, 'and it won't be no kiss.'

Della winked at Ellie. 'Promises, promises,' she said, grinning.

We had gone from serious to stupid in the space of one kiss. But we had nothing to laugh about. Things were going from bad to worse.

ELEVEN

The weather was getting worse. As we walked through the estate, past the concrete tower blocks, fat droplets of rain began to pound down. It took about three seconds before my hair was soaked and then the rest of my body followed suit. We passed the last tower block into the area by the side of the school, where a high chain fence separated the school grounds from a narrow alley-way, and the train tracks beyond it. The fence had holes in it all the way along and we stepped through one into the dark, wet alley. For some reason one of the Buju Banton tunes from the CD *Murderer* was playing over and over in my head in that weird way music sometimes does.

'Over there,' pointed Della, the rain streaming down her face.

To our left, where the alleyway ran round a corner towards its exit onto the main road, the wall was covered in graffiti. We headed towards it, hoping to find the stuff that had been written about Nanny. It was mostly tags for kids, all called things like Aces and Touch, but then we came across some really wicked art of a DJ playing his decks and I wondered how long it had taken the artist to do his work on that wall, and whether it had been pissing down at the time. The rainwater was disappearing down my neck onto my chest and back, and it was getting cold. I followed Will and Della as they moved along until we found what we were looking for.

'Here it is,' growled Will, more because of the rain than the writing on the wall.

It wasn't anywhere near the standard of the stuff I had just seen. There was only one colour and under a strange squiggle were the words NANNY IS A GRASS — BATTIE BWOI INFARMER — KILL DAT MAN. I wanted to laugh. I thought I'd be really angry, but the words had clearly been written by some fourteen-year-old dickhead. I put down the paint can I had with me and pulled a screwdriver from one of my jacket pockets, using it to lever the lid off. Then I got a paintbrush from my other pocket, which I'd found next to the paint in the shed, and began to paint over the offending words.

'I wish I knew who'd done that,' said Will.

'So you can give him spellin' lessons, you mean?' I replied.

'So I can kick his teeth down his throat – just before I strangle the knob,' he said.

'Jus' hurry up, will you,' complained Della. 'It's cold out here.'

I coated the words a few more times, daubing on the white paint quickly, and then, in a throwback to my youth, I threw the brush and the paint can over the wall.

'What'd you that for?' asked Della.

I shrugged. 'We used to tag this wall when I was about ten,' I told her. 'Just thought I was back there.'

'You ever hear his tag, sister?' Will asked her.

'No,' replied Della, 'and right now – me nuh care.'

'Rankin' B – my man thought he was a ragga star,' laughed Will.

'I could tell her about your first girlfriend . . .' I threatened.

'Easy – that's a bit too low, Billy. No need for that, my dan,' he replied quickly.

Della gave us both a hard look and then started off towards the main road. 'Yuh can buy me some fried chicken for this shit,' she told me.

'Fine by me, Dell.'

'Let's go get an umbrella first though. Rain's only getting worse.'

'Well, yuh can go two by two, like Noah an' him animals,' said Will. 'Some of us have to be on a building site at six in the morning.'

'Ouch!' I said.

'Least I go work,' said Will.

'Ooh you big *man*,' laughed Della, happier now that she knew she was getting some food. I didn't have a clue where she put it. She could eat five times a day and still not gain any weight.

'Kiss my beautiful black ass,' replied Will.

'Only if ouno gone clean de t'ing,' said Della.

Will grabbed her around the shoulders and gave her a bear hug.

'Man, what'd you do that for? You're all wet and nasty,' complained Della, when he let her go.

'You see? Don't mess with the size, sister,' he laughed, before leaving us at the corner of my street.

'Fool,' said Della as she watched him walk away.

We grabbed my mum's umbrella at my house and then walked arm in arm back to the main road and across to the shops down by the precinct. Even in the pouring rain there were people about: a gang of kids on bikes, an old wino sitting on the steps up to the library, and every now and then a car would pull over down the side streets and a dealer would appear from the shadows, do his thing and run back into the darkness. We walked past the precinct and down to another row of shops, to the fried chicken place with its red-and-blue sign and Urdu lettering on the window, just above posters for bargain meals and two-for-one fillet burgers. As we walked in, the owner smiled at me.

'Hello, Liverpool,' he said to me, in his thick Pakistani accent.

'All right,' I smiled back.

I had known him for years and he always called me Liverpool because he was a Manchester United fan himself. It was his way of taking the piss because his team were usually doing better than mine. Not that it bothered me. His fried chicken and hot wings were the best I'd ever tasted and he always gave me extra when he was around.

'Number one and eight wings twice,' I told him.

'With Diet Coke,' added Della. 'None of that full sugar shit.'

The owner grinned. 'For the lady an extra drink, I think,' he said.

Della smiled and then went to the door to shake out the umbrella.

'Your friend came in – five minutes since he gone,' the man told me.

'Which one?' I asked.

'Indian boy – Jas.'

'What, just now?'

'Yeah,' he replied, handing me two bags of food. I gave him a tenner and he returned five pounds in change, which was at least two quid too much.

'Thanks, bro.'

'No problem – your team doing better this year, innit?'

'We'll see,' I replied.

'Same old Liverpool.' He grinned. '*Salaam Alaikum.*'

'*Walaikum Salaam.*'

'Enjoy the food.'

'Yeah, I always do,' I told him, before heading back out into the rain.

'Back to mine?' I asked Della.

'Er yeah – unless we're gonna eat it in the rain.'

I was about to say something back when I saw a black Honda Accord pull up across the rain-soaked street: Jas got out of the passenger side.

'*Jas!*' I shouted.

Della turned and looked over at her boyfriend. Jas looked up and then leaned into the car and spoke to the driver. He shut the door and ran over to us.

'All right,' he said.

'Fuck me – it's a ghost,' I said.

'I thought you were gonna call me,' said Della.

'I was just about to,' replied Jas. 'Just finished doin' some stuff for Dee.'

'That your cousin?' I asked, even though I knew it was.

'Yeah, I'm working with him – his old man owns a clothing factory,' he told me.

'Funny time to finish work,' said Della.

'Late delivery that we had to get sorted for tomorrow,' Jas told her.

'So where you been?' I asked, hoping that Jas and Della weren't about to have a row in the street.

'Around, man,' he replied, looking up and down the street.

'But not answering your phone?'

He shrugged. 'Things to do, Billy. I'm working now and things are busy, you get me.'

'So busy you can't reply to a text even?' I continued.

'Don't be like that, man. We're not kids no more.'

'I thought we was mates, that's all,' I told him.

'We are mates, bro – always will be. It's just that I wanna get to know my family and that – make some money.'

I nodded. 'Still don't see why you can't call us now and then.'

Jas looked at Della, who looked away. 'I will,' he said.

'There's some shit happenin',' I said. 'Stuff to do with what happened before . . .'

I was going to continue but Jas didn't seem interested. He kept on looking over at his cousin's car. Then his phone went off. He answered it and told the caller that he was coming.

'Gotta go,' he said, with a sniff. 'I'll call you tomorrow, bro – promise.'

'Cool,' I said.

Jas turned to Della. 'Just got a few more bits to do and then I'll call you,' he told her.

'I'm going to Billy's,' replied Della. 'And then I'm going to bed. Got an early start in the morning.'

'I'll still call you,' insisted Jas.

Della looked at him with no emotion in her eyes. Not even anger. 'Do what you like,' she told him before walking off towards my house.

I shrugged.

'Maybe you two should chat,' I said.

'Nah,' Jas grinned. 'It's nuttin'.'

'Well I'm goin' after her,' I told him.

'Yeah . . . Look, I'll bell you tomorrow – for definite,' he said.

'You'd better,' I replied, smiling.

He turned, ran back to the car and got in. His

shaven-headed cousin said something to him and then looked at me. He started the car and drove off, pulling up about a hundred metres down the road. I watched them for a moment and then set off after Della.

TWELVE

Jas didn't bother to call Della that night and he failed to get in touch with me the next day. I put it down to him being busy but part of me was hurt and a little bit angry at the way he was acting. I was slamming trays of French bread dough into racks, ready to wheel into the large ovens at work, as I thought about it. After the fifth rack my line manager, a knob called Paul, asked me what was up.

'Nuttin',' I told him.

'Well don't take it out on the racks – that's company equipment, son,' he told me, like he owned the store rather than just worked for it – on crap money.

'Whatever . . .' I replied, wheeling the racks into the oven.

'I need you to do overtime this week, Billy. To make up for all the shifts you've missed.'

'Can't do it,' I told him flatly.

'You've not even seen the rota yet,' he said.

'Don't care — I do my twenty-five hours and then I'm gone.'

'But I'm gonna be left with no one to cover the early shift on Wednesday and the area manager's coming in,' he pleaded.

For a minute I thought about it. The extra money. Then he showed me the shift on the rota. I would have to get in by four in the morning and do the so-called master baker's job — a total of three extra hours which were worth about twelve quid to me. I shook my head.

'You'll have to get one of the others to cover,' I said.

'But—'

'Or you could do it yerself,' I reminded him. 'I'm off for my break anyhow.'

And with that I left Paul to lose his hair and raise his blood pressure over his precious rota.

I walked out at the end of my shift and turned on my new mobile, crossing the busy dual carriage-way in front of the store to go and wait for a bus back into the city centre. I had two messages. The first was from Ellie, making sure that I remembered I was going into the school. The second was from Will. He had finished for the day because of some problem on the site he was working at. I rang him and arranged to grab him on my way to see Ellie. His mum, who suffered from arthritis and was mostly house-bound, was going to a day care centre at twelve, and he was free after that. Will's dad had taken advantage of Will being at home to go and sort out a claim at the job centre.

As I waited for my bus I thought a bit more about Jas and the blatant way in which he had lied to me and Della. I knew that people often said they'd call and didn't but Jas wasn't people. He was like family, and when the people you love let you down, it hurts much more and makes you that much angrier. When it became clear that Jas wasn't going to call, Della rang her foster mum Sue to tell her that she was staying at mine and turned off her phone. Then she fell asleep on my bed and was gone before I got up for work, without saying a word. She was *angry*.

The bus dropped me off at the edge of the ring road that circled around the city centre and I walked slowly across the iron bridge behind the train station and up the main road, back to my mum's. It was a grey day, one of those overcast ones, and there was slight chill in the air. I passed a couple of homeless drunks by a little park down a side street that ran parallel with mine and one of them swerved into my path. I stepped aside to avoid him and felt something slide underneath my foot. I looked down and swore. It was a used condom. The drunks thought that I was swearing at them and started to get aggressive but I ignored them and cussed silently all the way to my front door. Once I got in, I changed my trainers and washed the soles of the ones I'd been wearing. Then I put on a hooded fleece top to keep out the cold, drank a glass of orange juice and left to call for Will.

Ellie was waiting for us at the school gates, her hair up on her head and a big warm smile on her face, as well as a look of relief in her eyes.

'Hey, Baby – you OK?' I asked, giving her a hug.

'Yeah,' she replied, before saying hello to Will.

'So where these bwoi at?' he asked, ready to get down to business.

'They go over by the precinct at lunch,' Ellie told us.

I walked into the school grounds and looked around a bit. It was exactly the same as always, with its battered doors and fading sign above the reception area. The pupils were just milling around everywhere – from Year Sevens, who looked to me like they were infants, to the Year Tens and Elevens, who acted as if they ran the place, just like I had when I'd been there – before they'd thrown me out.

'That Shields still the principal?' asked Will.

'Yeah – although there's a new deputy this year,' replied Ellie. 'Big scary-looking bloke with huge muscles . . .'

'Oh yeah?' said an interested Will as he flexed his thigh-sized biceps. 'Big as mine?'

Ellie grinned. 'Makes you look like Bart Simpson – if he was black, that is.'

'You cheeky likkle raas,' laughed Will.

'What's he called, this new bloke?' I asked.

'Manners.'

'And he's here to teach them too, right?' I continued.

'Of course – that's all he ever says: *My ambition is the same as my name*,' she mimicked in a deep voice.

A gang of five girls had gathered at the door into the school and were looking at us.

'They mates of yours?' asked Will.

Ellie glanced round, saw the girls and then turned back again. 'No, they're part of the gang that pick on me,' she said, going red in the face.

'Not no more they ain't,' I told her. 'Wait here with Will.'

I walked over to the girls slowly. As I

approached one of them stepped forward with a frown on her face.

'What you *want*?' she spat at me.

I pointed at Ellie. 'See her there – she's off limits, sister. No more giving her shit,' I told her.

'Or *what*?' asked the girl, her eyes blazing.

'Or I'll get my friend Della to pay you sisters a visit,' I told them all. 'You remember her from last *year*?'

The girls all looked at each other and one or two seemed scared. It didn't surprise me. Della had the *boys* under manners at the school when she was there – never mind the girls.

'I don't listen to no informer,' said the first girl.

'And yuh can stop with that nonsense an' all,' I replied.

'Yuh think no one know yuh? Grassin' up *all* dem man?'

I gave her a dirty look and then smiled. 'Whatever, sister – I ain't got no problem wit' you. Just leave my friend alone – and anyone you hear callin' me or my crew things – yuh just tell them to come knock on my door, *y'hear*?'

'Might jus' do that,' sneered the girl.

'Say hello to Della when she finds you,' I said, before turning to walk off.

Behind me the girl kissed her teeth and called me a few names. I ignored her. I didn't want to get into a slanging match with some idiot girl at Ellie's school.

'Yuh handle that well,' teased Will.

'What was I *supposed* to do – beat her up? Men don't touch women – not *proper* men.'

'I didn't say that, bro,' replied Will. 'But you could have used the D-Bomb on 'em.'

The D-Bomb was Della.

'I did,' I told him, grinning.

I turned to Ellie. 'Next time that blabbermout' says anything to you – tell Della,' I said to her.

'OK,' replied Ellie, looking unsure.

As if we had sent out a signal across the airwaves straight to her head, Della walked up from the direction of the precinct and the community centre.

'Tell me what?' she demanded.

'*Bastard!*' said a shocked Will. 'What are you – a ghost?'

'Tell me *what*?' repeated Della, looking at me and not Ellie. She wasn't going to repeat herself a second time.

I nodded in the direction of the group of girls and told Della what had gone on.

'The mouthy one is Leah,' Della told us. 'I'm surprised she's still here.'

Then, without another word, Della walked calmly over to the group of girls, grabbed Leah by her neck and whispered something in her ear. The other girls stepped back. Leah listened and when Della let her go, she hung her head and walked after her mates. Della turned and came back over to us.

'What did you say to her?' asked Ellie.

'Never mind, baby girl — just don't be expecting no more trouble from her. Now let's go find the lads too,' replied Della.

I looked at Will and shook my head.

'*D-Bomb*, man,' laughed Will. 'Gets dem every time — no prisoners, seen?'

THIRTEEN

We left Ellie at the school and set off towards the shops. The lads we were after were standing on a street corner, halfway between the precinct and the school. The street was narrow and they watched us as we approached them. I recognized most of them: they were youths from around the area – I even knew some of them. But none of that mattered at that point. The only thing that concerned me was that they had been picking on Ellie and they were going to stop. Then I saw the lad from the night we'd gone to speak to Gary at the community centre, when we were looking for the lads who had mugged me. He stepped up as we approached, smirking. Something in his face was more than just familiar but I couldn't work out what it was.

I tensed up as we drew closer.

'Here come the famous five,' shouted one of the lads, without showing his face.

Will let out a little growl and clenched his jaw muscles. I could tell that he was on a short fuse. I decided to step up and try and stop any violence. If they had any sense they would just listen and leave it anyway.

'You've been pickin' on our friend,' I told them. 'Callin' us grasses and t'ing. It ain't right.'

Most of the lads looked away, at their feet or at each other. One of them – a lad called Sean – spat on the ground and then cleared his throat.

'So?' He shrugged.

'So – either yuh stop, Sean, or I'm gonna mash up your face so bad even yuh mother won't want to know yer,' threatened Della.

Sean smirked and looked at the lad from the night before. The lad was staring straight at me.

'Yuh like pickin' on kids or summat?' he said to me.

'Same as you do, I guess,' I replied.

There was definitely something in his face that I recognized although if he carried on the way he was going, it wasn't going to be there for much longer.

'Ain't no one here picking on no one,' said Sean. 'And it ain't like you *ain't* tellin' the police stuff – *everyone* in the neighbourhood knows it – it's all over, man.'

'Well it's a fucking lie and man ain't gonna live to repeat it,' snapped Della.

'Ain't our fault you can't tek the truth – no need for trouble 'cos of that,' said Sean, smirking again.

'Wrong,' replied Will, smashing his open palm into the side of Sean's head and sending him sprawling to the floor. So much for being the peacemaker, I thought to myself.

Most of the gang took a step back and left it, but the lad that had it in for me took a swing at my head. I ducked inside his punch and caught him right under his ribcage with a fist. He doubled over, unable to breathe properly. Then Will grabbed him around his middle and gave him a bear hug before throwing him into the street. One of the other lads stepped up but caught a slap from Della. He held his face, lip split on his teeth, and began to cry.

'*Enough!!*' I heard from behind us.

We turned to see Nanny sprinting in our direction. Despite that, I grabbed the lad I'd hit and threatened him.

'Next time – I'll fuck your face right up. Don't think we is soft just cause we don't like to hang on street corners no more, bwoi,' I spat at him.

He mumbled something that I ignored.

'We been deh 'bout fe a long time – ain't

no likkle bwoi crew gonna tell we nuttin',' I added.

I let him go just as Nanny arrived, his face like thunder.

'What de pussyclaat a gwan yah?' he demanded.

I just shrugged.

It was only later that I started to feel a little bit ashamed for fighting in the street like an idiot. Will and Della were sitting opposite me in my mum's kitchen and we were trying to explain what had happened to Nanny. I felt like I used to when I was thirteen and getting into trouble every other night over one thing or another. I knew that fighting was the wrong thing to do – it was what I believed, but my beliefs and my actions often didn't meet. And that made me feel foolish. But where we lived things sometimes went a particular way: even if you didn't want to end up scrapping, somehow you did. It was just the way things were sometimes. And this time we had very good reasons too, or at least that was what we were telling Nanny.

'What *reason*?' he asked. 'Man and man war all over de world – dem always claim seh dem have a reason.'

'But—' I began.

Nanny shook his head. 'Reason and war is not

compatible, yuh unnerstan'? Is no *reason* to fight pon de streets – yuh nuh 'fraid fe yuh life. Yuh not hungry. No man a bulldoze yuh home an' tek way yuh rights – is what *reason* yuh have fe fight?'

'They was callin' us things,' said Della. 'Picking on the baby girl.'

'That's a reason to fight?' asked Nanny.

'But you don't know what they were saying, Nanny,' added Will.

'That's why me ask yuh de question,' replied Nanny.

I looked at the other two and decided that we had to tell Nanny everything.

'They've been writing shit on the walls,' I began. 'Calling you a grass. Threatening Ellie at school—'

'Who?' asked Nanny. 'Dem yout', man?'

'Yeah . . .'

'*So?*' he asked with a shrug.

'But people are whispering stuff like that about all of us – it ain't good,' said Will.

'Dem yout's,' said Nanny. 'Just messin' about. Ain't nuttin' *serious.*'

'It is if you're Ellie and you're being picked on,' said Della.

'But yuh can *talk* about dem t'ings – mek dem unnerstan' yuh words—'

'And if the words don't work?' she asked.

'Den let them talk. If dem want *bark* like dog – let dem *bark*,' he said, shaking his head.

'But everyone else is going to think we're informers,' I reminded him. 'People are getting arrested all over the place and *we're* getting the blame. Can't you *see* how dangerous that is?'

'Let dem bark, Billy,' he repeated. 'The people we know, *know* us. Dem never gonna believe no rumours.'

'But what if they *do*?' asked Will. 'What if they do and we get more shit because of it?'

'Then – if man threaten we family or we house – then we have reason to fight,' he told us. 'But dis is not *serious*.'

I shrugged. 'Maybe you're right, Nan,' I said to him. 'But someone had to put them knobs in their place.'

He looked at me with a tinge of disappointment in his eyes. 'Well, you've done that,' he said quietly. 'Now yuh feel like a big man?'

I didn't reply and Nanny left us sitting there and went out. I looked at the other two and smiled.

'They won't be saying nothing to Ellie anyway,' I said.

'Too right,' agreed Della.

'I can see what he means though,' added Will. 'I feel a bit ashamed now . . .'

'Yeah, me too,' I admitted.

'Well – I'm hungry,' said Della.

Will grinned. 'Man, you is always eating. One day it's gonna catch you up and you'll be on morning telly talking 'bout you used to be fifty kilos and now yuh is over five hundred,' he joked.

'I thought you were supposed to be at college anyway?' I added.

Della shrugged. 'Didn't go. Weren't in the mood,' she replied, looking at me. I understood. Jas was the reason she didn't go in.

I stood up and said I'd find something in the fridge. I still felt foolish and ashamed and I tried hard not to feel that way. I didn't know it but my mood was about to change anyway. Sometimes when you cover and heat a pot of water, it only boils over. Other times the lid rattles. In our case, the lid was about to blow clean off.

FOURTEEN

Divy thought quickly as he stood with his back to the school gates. He listened to Dee on the other end of his mobile phone and nodded, as though Dee was actually there with him.

'Cool,' said Divy. 'I'll be over in about half an hour. I've just gotta take me mum to the shop, man. You know how it is . . .'

He listened as Dee complained and told him to get his fat arse over to their meeting as quickly as he could. Divy said he'd be there as soon as and flipped his phone shut.

'Dickhead,' he muttered to himself as he heard the kids begin to leave school for the day.

He stood and watched them for another five minutes before Sean came sauntering out with his mate Tyrone in tow. As they got closer, Divy saw the huge bruise on the side of Sean's face.

'What the *raas* happened to you?' he asked.

Sean looked around and then told Divy about his run-in with Will, Billy and Della. Divy listened and nodded.

'They touch *you*?' Divy asked Tyrone.

'Yeah – that Billy had a pop at me but don't worry – he'll get his,' replied Tyrone.

'Never mind about that, rude boy – you didn't tell them anything, did you?'

Sean shook his head. 'Nah – we just told 'em what you said to – and then Billy's dad turned up.'

'That dreadlocked, Bob Marley looking wanker?'

'*Yeah* – Nanny . . .' said Sean.

'*He* do anything?' asked Divy.

'He shouted at them and took them off home,' grinned Sean. 'Like he had to protect us from them – the *knob*.'

Divy thought about his instructions. 'And this was all 'cos you been picking on the blonde?' he said.

Sean nodded. 'Yeah – that's all they was on about. They don't know *shit* about that other stuff.'

'Good,' replied Divy. 'Make sure it stays that way an' all.'

Sean opened his bag and handed Divy a mobile phone. Divy looked at it and then dialled his own phone from it. He held his own open and waited for the number to appear on its screen. Then he stored it before putting the stolen phone away with his own.

'Nice,' he said.

'You want us to carry on with the blonde?' asked Tyrone.

'No,' replied Divy, remembering what he'd been told. The whisper was the important thing. Once it got started it would take on a life of its own.

'So that's it?' asked Sean.

'Nah, bro, there's more.'

'You got my payment first?' demanded Sean.

'I got an eighth for yer – you can get at least seven gs out of that, if you do like I said and cut it. Depends on how much is going up yer own nose, bro.'

Sean grinned. 'Nice,' he said. 'Man and man waitin' on that shit.'

Divy passed him a wrap of cocaine and then looked at Tyrone. 'I got you the same,' he told him.

Tyrone shook his head. 'Nah man – I ain't into that t'ing deh. Strictly cash me a deal wid, blood.'

Divy looked at him for a minute, as he considered whether he should just kick his head in. Who was he anyway? Some new bwoi in the area – making demands like he ran the place. Then he remembered something else that he'd been warned about. No mess. Just get it done. On the quiet. He forced a smile and reached into his back pocket to pull out his cash. Peeling off one hundred quid, he handed it to Tyrone.

'There you go, Tee. Don't spend it all at once.'

Tyrone pocketed the cash before he replied. 'So what you want us to do next?' he asked.

Divy was late for his meeting with Dee on purpose. They were standing in the middle of Victoria Park in the freezing cold, with the darkness closing in, waiting for him. Dee, Jas, Kully and another bloke: Divy realized this was Malk, the third brother, who he hadn't met yet.

'Easy,' he said as he approached them.

'Don't speak,' barked Kully.

Divy watched him step forward and for a second thought that he was being ambushed. He realized he was safe when Kully told him he was gonna be searched.

'For *what*, man – *tape recorder*?' asked Divy, as a joke.

Kully glared at him. 'Don't even start with that,' he told him. 'Four more street dealers got nicked today – one of them works for us.'

'Well it ain't *me* chatting to no police.'

'I'm still gonna check you out,' said Kully.

Divy held up his arms like he saw it done on the telly and waited as Kully searched him. As he finished he gave Dee a nod.

'From now on you talk only to Jas and me,' Dee said.

'I thought that's what was happenin' anyway,' replied Divy.

'It is,' snapped Kully. 'We're just making it clear, Divy. You're like *us*, man, Punjabi, so maybe we trust you more than them other man we got dealing on the streets.'

'*And?*' asked Divy.

'And that means that from now on you and Jas are running the *whole* street thing for us, with Dee as your contact,' continued Kully.

'Fine by me,' said Divy, fighting off an urge to grin.

'And we want you to find out who's talkin' to the coppers – if you hear *anything*, you let Dee know,' added Kully.

'But if you're playing us,' said Malk, stepping forward, right into Divy's face, 'then' – Divy watched, frozen, as the biggest of the brothers pulled a silver handgun from his pocket and held it to his head – 'you and your entire family are dead. You understand me, Divinder? *All* of them . . .'

Divy nodded slowly and tried not to lose control of his bladder. Malk put the gun away and walked off into the darkness, towards the main road.

'Don't worry about him,' laughed Kully. 'We only get him out to scare the madmen.'

Divy sighed deeply, took a breath and forced a smile. 'No problem, bro,' he told Kully. 'I understand, man. Gotta protect what's yours.'

'Exactly,' agreed Dee.

Divy looked over at Jas. He was staring away into the distance.

'You happy working with me, rudes?' Divy asked him.

Jas looked at him and shrugged. 'Yeah . . .'

'Time to put the past behind us, bro – stick to we own kind,' added Divy.

'That's *exactly* what's gonna stop us from getting done like all them other man,' said Kully.

Divy smiled and decided that it was time to give his boss another call.

'We're goin' down a new bar we got some money in – if you wanna join us,' Kully said to him.

'Yeah, man,' replied Divy. 'I could get me some of that.'

FIFTEEN

The following day things started to get seriously bad. It started out like any other day. I finished work at two and came home to find Nanny deep in conversation with one of his Rastafarian friends, a bloke called Nyah, who was talking about his forthcoming trip to Africa. It turned out that he was going to help build a school in Ethiopia, and to try and get used to the life over there.

'An' if Jah want it — I man ago tek my woman and move out permanently,' he told Nanny.

'Sister Corinne happy 'bout that?' asked Nanny.

'Yeah man — she's comin' out to help wid the school.'

'Seen,' replied Nanny.

'One day you ago check fe me and yuh nah go find me,' grinned Nyah.

'Could always come over for a holiday,' I suggested.

'Yeah man – when me build my villa.'

I was about to say he should add a pool too but Nanny told me that they were going out.

'Can yuh get the dinner started, man – just fry off some onion and t'ing – get the masala ready?' he asked.

'Yeah – anything else?'

'Nah – I'll get the okra in town and me have sweet potato already,' he replied.

'OK – I'll see you both later then,' I said.

'Irie,' replied Nyah.

'Oh, and Ellie left you a message to go round later,' added Nanny.

'Cool.'

After I'd done the masala, ready for the okra curry Nanny was going to make, I showered and then hooked up to the Internet. I was just surfing, looking at all kinds of sites, killing time because I was bored. At one point I hit a site with loads of pop-ups and had to spend ages just shutting them down, one after the other. It was a real pain. In the end I logged off and went downstairs to watch TV, which was even worse. Every programme was about people selling their possessions to buy other stuff or people being walked around big houses in Spain and Italy that they couldn't afford. I think I fell asleep because the next thing I knew my mum was home from work and waking me up, a tired look on her face.

'Ain't you got anything better to do with your day?' she asked me, after I'd rubbed my eyes for a bit and worked out what was going on.

'No,' I answered truthfully. I couldn't think of a single thing that I really had to do.

'Well, you could have tidied the yard, like I asked you to. You could have cleaned the kitchen and the bathroom – both of which are disgusting, by the way,' she told me.

'*Mum*—'

'Well there's always *something* to do, Billy – other than sleep. Justify your existence for a change. Mop the kitchen floor—'

'Man – I wish I'd stayed at work,' I complained.

'Even that would be preferable,' my mum told me. 'Can't you extend your hours or something – go full time?'

'Sack that – I'd rather pull my own teeth out.'

She smiled. 'Or I could do it for you, you lazy little shit,' she said.

'*Mum!*'

'And look, you've dribbled on the cushions,' she continued.

She couldn't have picked a worse time to say what she did as Ellie had just walked in.

'*Ehh!* You dirty little—' said Ellie.

'Hi, Ellie,' smiled my mum.

'Hi.'

'Man – you got your own key or something?' I asked Ellie.

'Well, actually, yes she has,' said my mum. 'She's always round here so I thought it would make sense if she just let herself in.'

'So that I can secretly watch you while you sleep,' Ellie told me. 'Drool over you as you dribble—'

'Oh great – I was in the shower earlier. You could have walked in on me,' I complained.

Ellie mumbled something under her breath that only my mum heard. She gave Ellie a surprised look and then shook her head.

'What's she say?' I asked.

'Oh . . . nothing,' grinned my mum. 'Girl stuff . . .'

Ellie beamed at my mum and then stuck her tongue out at me.

'What do you want *anyway*?' I asked her.

'Ooh, listen to Mr Charm – I was going to ask if you'd walk to the supermarket with me? I've got to do some shopping for my mum.' She put on her pleading voice.

'Which one?' I asked.

'The big one, on the way into town.'

'That's miles away,' I complained.

'Oh shut up, you girl – it's only ten minutes' walk,' she told me.

'More like twenty . . .'

'Fifteen then,' she said, smiling her cutest smile, which got me every time.

'Oh – all right then,' I agreed.

We walked through the ghetto and down towards the ring road, past a retail park with the worst selection of shops ever. It was like the person who'd decided to build it had thought, *I know – I'll take all the shops that no one likes and bung them all together on the arsehole end of town – that'll pick up business.* Ellie had her arm in mine and she was walking really slowly, so that I had to keep checking my steps. I didn't mind though.

'So they leave you alone at school today?' I asked her.

'Yeah. The lads didn't even look at me and Leah didn't come to school at all.'

'Good,' I told her.

'I dunno what Della said to her but it worked.'

'Best leave that to Della,' I said, grinning. 'She can be scary when she wants to be.'

'No she can't. She's so beautiful – she even looks pretty when she cries,' said Ellie.

I gave her a funny look. 'She been crying a lot then?' I asked.

'*Oops*,' said Ellie. 'Oh look, there's an elephant with only one leg—'

'Ellie . . .' I said sternly.

'Oh all right then – she told me not to say anything but . . .' She paused for a moment – just long enough to wind me up.

'*But?*' I demanded.

'Well – you know how Jas is being really mean to her?'

'Yeah – she told me about all that,' I told her.

'Well, she's split up with him. In her head, I mean. And now she's upset because she's going to have to tell him and he won't be happy and it'll all end in tears and—'

'OK, Baby, I get the point.'

'So she's been crying a lot and still looking great but she loves him and when you love someone and they don't love you back – it's really horrible. I should know.'

I gave her another funny look. 'You in love with someone who doesn't love you back?' I asked. 'I didn't even know you had a boyfriend.'

Ellie turned my favourite shade of red. Liverpool FC red. 'Er . . . not now – ages ago, when I was younger and—'

'Ellie's telling porkies,' I teased.

'No I'm not!' she snapped. 'It was a slip of the tongue. I . . . er . . . didn't mean to say me exactly.'

'Forget it, Ellie – I was only teasing you.'

She pinched my arse really hard.

'*Oww!*'

'Serves you right for being such a git,' she told me.

We spent twenty minutes in the supermarket, buying veg and stuff for Ellie's mum. As we walked around the aisles, Ellie rode on the back of the trolley so that her bum stuck out, like she always did, and at the till she asked the cashier if they had any jobs for people who couldn't hear properly because she knew an old man called Billy who needed a proper job. The cashier said no and gave me a look that made me feel like I was some kind of nonce. It was that 'she's young and you look old so what are you doing together' thing. I mean, there was only two years between us anyway but the fact that Ellie had such a baby face meant that lots of people thought she was younger. Not that it was any of the cashier's business anyhow. I got so pissed off that I leaned over and kissed Ellie on the cheek. The woman's eyes nearly popped out of her head – stupid old bag.

We walked home, but as we turned the corner into our street we realized that something was wrong. Police sirens were wailing in the distance. The bins had been turned over all the way down and everyone was outside their houses. When we got to Ellie's house, her parents were looking at what used to be their car. It had been trashed and set on fire.

I looked over at my mum's house and that was when I saw the broken windows and what looked like shit smeared down the door. There was a bit of paper, a note, taped to the gate-post that nobody seemed to have noticed. I pulled it off and read it.

It said: '*Bang, bang – Informer man dead.*'

SIXTEEN

My mum came down the street from the direction of the alley that ran behind our house, and I was shocked to see DI Elliot with her. I stuffed the note into my pocket. I didn't want Elliot to see it. We were in enough shit already, with people calling us informers. The last thing we needed was for them to see the note too. It would have given the whisper a ring of truth that it didn't deserve. And one that we couldn't afford.

My mum looked shocked and Elliot was on her phone. I turned and walked over to Ellie's dad: his face was red with anger.

'What the hell happened, Mr Sykes?' I asked.

'I heard a load of banging and then glass smashing and when I got outside the bloody car was on fire,' he told me through clenched teeth. 'I've got a fire extinguisher in the shed, from the garage, and I used it to put most of the flames out. It smells like a petrol bomb.'

I'd only ever seen him that angry once before and that was when Ellie had been kidnapped. I asked him if he'd seen anyone.

'A bunch of kids,' he said. 'Wearin' baseball caps and baggy jeans. They ran off that way.' He pointed in the direction from which my mum and Elliot had returned.

'The little bastards,' he growled. 'Wait until I get hold of them.'

'Where's Nanny?' I asked.

'He's gone after them,' he replied.

Ellie and her mum were crying and I took them inside and told them to try and calm down. And then I asked Christopher, Ellie's brother, if he was OK.

'Yeah. I was upstairs on the computer,' he told me.

'So you didn't see anything?'

He looked worried. 'Er . . . no.'

'It's all right, Chris — you're not in trouble,' I reassured him.

'OK,' he said, smiling.

I left him with his mum and sister and went back out. Looking up and down the street, I saw that although there was quite a lot of mess around, only our two houses seemed to have been damaged in any way. Even without the note, I would have known straight away that it was down to the whisper that was going round about us – that we were grasses. What else could it mean? I looked at DI Elliot and thought about telling her what was on my mind. But she was the reason we were in this mess. If we hadn't involved the police when we had all the trouble with Busta, we wouldn't have been labelled grasses and none of this would have happened. And it didn't help that she'd called round to see my mum either. Someone was playing us and they were doing a good job.

My mum came up to me and asked me if I was OK.

'Yeah, I'm fine – I'm just waiting for Nanny,' I told her.

'He's gone after them,' she told me.

'Yeah, Ellie's dad told me. Who was it?'

'Just a bunch of kids,' she replied. 'There's been a few incidents like this recently.'

'Funny how they all seem to be targeting us,' I said.

My mum gave me a questioning look. 'It's not just us – look at Brian's car,' she said.

'I meant them as well,' I told her.

'And the rest of the street, too,' she reminded me.

'Yeah, but they ain't had *their* cars burned or *their* windows put through – this is all about us.'

Only my mum dismissed what I'd said and told

me that I was being overly paranoid. It was just a bunch of kids with nothing better to do. A load of yobs. And then she went over to DI Elliot, just as two police cars came speeding down the road, with their lights flashing. Just what we needed. More false evidence for whoever was pointing the finger at us. Suddenly I wondered if the people who had done it were watching and I began to scan the gathering crowd for faces that seemed odd. But they were only in my head, those odd faces. The crowd was full of people we knew, neighbours and friends. I watched as the coppers began to question them about what had happened, and a fire engine turned up to check Ellie's dad's car, which was smoking rather than on fire by now.

I saw Nanny striding down the road and as he approached I pulled him to one side.

'Believe us *now*?' I said.

'Wha' yuh a chat 'bout?' he asked.

'The rumours, Nan. People callin' us informers – that's what this is about.'

'Just hol' dem theory till we know what a gwan, Billy.'

'But . . .' I began, only for Nanny to go over to Ellie's dad and start talking to him instead.

I started to feel paranoid and stupid and then I remembered the note I'd put in my pocket. I was right. I pulled out my phone and rang Will and then Della, asking them to come over if they could. We'd see who was being paranoid.

It took until one in the morning for the wreck that was Mr Sykes's car to be taken away and for our broken windows to be fixed. DI Elliot had called a man that she knew to come and change them quickly and on the cheap, and she didn't leave until the job was done. As she left the house, I realized that anyone watching would think that we were best friends with a detective. It looked bad. I told Will and Della as much.

'You're right,' said Will.

'We need to show Nanny that note,' added Della.

'I'll go and get him in a minute,' I told them.

'I can't believe that Elliot didn't see the note though,' said Will. 'Ain't that what she's about – *detectin*'?'

'They must have rushed out or summat,' said Della.

'The note *was* taped to the fence-post so maybe they didn't see it,' I said. 'It would have been below their line of sight—'

'Easy – check out Mr CID,' grinned Will.

'This ain't funny, big man,' I replied. 'Someone's got it in for us and we ain't got a clue who it is.'

'Yeah we do – it's them lads we battered the other day,' argued Will.

I shook my head. 'They're *boys* – they might be doing stuff 'cos they've heard some rumour but they ain't the ones who started it. That's gotta be someone else,' I said.

Della nodded. 'Billy's right, y'know. Them lads ain't got the brains for nuttin' like this. But I still don't get who it might be.'

'What if some big mouth has just spread a whisper and it's got out of hand?' asked Will.

'That's possible,' agreed Della.

'But *someone* must actually be telling the police stuff – all them dealers ain't getting sent down 'cos the Babylon took clever pills for a change,' I said to them.

'True,' nodded Will.

'So who's doing the informing? And if we can find *them* maybe we can stop people chatting fuckery about us,' I continued.

'Yeah, but half the bad man in the city is lookin' fe dem man,' Will pointed out. 'How *we* gonna find them?'

In my head I said the word 'contacts' but I didn't speak it out loud. I was going to get hold of Lynden in the morning to see if he knew anything. Check up on what he'd found out about Jas and his new friends.

'Lemme go get Nanny,' I told them.

I found Nanny standing by the front door.

'Nanny – there's something we need to talk to you about,' I told him.

'*We?*' he asked, with a slight smile.

'Me, Will and Della.'

'Seen . . .'

He followed me back into the living room and sat down next to Della.

'So what yuh have to tell me?' he asked, loosening his dreads and letting them fall onto his shoulders.

'This attack is about the whispers,' I began.

I thought Nanny would tell me to shut up or something but he looked thoughtful instead.

'Go on,' he said.

'When I got back from the supermarket, when you went after them kids, I found something taped to the gate. A note . . .'

I pulled it out of my pocket and handed it to him. Nanny took it and read it. Then he sat and looked at it for a while before anyone spoke. I could hear the clock on the wall ticking.

'The policewoman tell yuh muddah dat we should look into one a dem ASBO t'ing—' he told me.

'A *what*?' asked Della.

'An anti-social behaviour order,' replied Will.

'It's one of the stupid things that stops kids from playing in the street.'

'What did Mum say?' I asked Nanny.

'Nuttin' much,' he said with a shrug. 'But this note mek t'ings more serious.'

'It's all about the whole informer thing,' I told him. 'Yesterday, when we grabbed them lads – the night before we went to get rid of some graffiti about you—'

'About *me*?' he said, in shock.

'Yeah – them lads wrote it in that alley down between the school and railway tracks . . .'

I told him what it had said and he sat and played with his beard for a bit.

'We need to get them lads again and find out who's behind all of this,' insisted Will.

Nanny shook his head and spoke softly. 'Let me go and check some a mi bredren dem. In de mornin'. If deh is anyt'ing goin' on – me will find out.'

'But we want to help with it,' I told him.

'Help me by leavin' it alone, Billy,' he said. 'I man can deal wid it – in a way dat won't stress yuh muddah—'

'But—' began Della.

'But nuttin',' replied Nanny gently. 'Me ago deal wid it an' dis time we nah go check fe no dutty Babylon.'

We had all grown used to Nanny and his ways, and when he said things softly, that's when we listened. He wasn't going to let us argue about it. But we *should* have argued. We should have thought things through a bit more, connected the dots. Tried to find out who was saying stuff. Maybe even involved DI Elliot. Maybe then things would have turned out differently. But that night we set ourselves on a course that was going to lead to danger and death. Like we had decided to sail through rocks with a blindfold on.

PHONE CALL

'What's happenin', Divy?'

'Everything goin' to plan.'

'So you're in with the brothers?'

'Yeah – I even met the oldest one, Malk. He's nuts.'

'And the kids?'

'They got a shock last night – some fireworks and a nice note.'

'What about the next bit?'

'Yeah – that's sorted too. We'll get them out on the street as soon as you give the say-so, B.'

'Get them out tonight then – no point letting them think they're in the clear. And then let's get the other side up and running. I want you to find out when the brothers are making their next big pick-up. Get everything you can and then pass it on—'

'I still don't get it, B.'

'You leave the scheming to me, Divy. Just do like I say, and when things are back to normal – you're my partner. Set up for life, my yout'.'

'You better remember that too, B. This shit ain't easy. That nutter Malk put a piece to my head the other night.'

'Oh yeah? Then maybe he's the one we'll give to the beast.'

'Yeah — that's what we should do.'

'Them kids you're using — they don't know too much, do they?'

'Nah — they think that Billy and his mates are the grasses. They ain't got a clue.'

'Nice.'

'Anything else, B?'

'Yeah — after the next step — before we get to that dreadlocked pussyhole, I want you to call me. I wanna tell you exactly what to do, you get me?'

'Anything you say, boss.'

'That bwoi is gonna pay big time. Ain't no amount of chanting to Jah gonna help that man.'

SEVENTEEN

Jas looked at himself in the mirror. His eyes were red and the bags under them almost purple. He ran the cold tap and washed his face, hoping to feel a bit more human, but the freezing water just made him feel worse. His nostrils were burning and no matter how often he blew his nose, it felt like there was something permanently lodged in his sinuses. He walked back to his bedroom, relieved that his mum was at work already. Next to his bed sat his phone, his cash and his stash. He picked up the drugs and looked at them over and over. Then he walked over to his CD player, put in a Method Man disc and turned it on. For a few moments the familiar beat felt right in his head but then it started to thump and take over his thoughts and he felt his head beginning to vibrate. The vibration headed down into his sinuses and he sniffed again. He got up, turned off the CD and went back to his bed.

He lay there for about half an hour, trying to will himself to sleep, but all he could hear was the noise from outside his window and his clock ticking. Ticking. Ticking. He got up again and took the clock into the bathroom. He went back into his bedroom, shut the door and pulled the curtains as close together as they would go. Then he got back into bed. He remembered seeing some programme about using deep breathing to relax and tried to follow the instructions he could recall. He lay on his back, perfectly flat with his arms at his sides, and closed his eyes. Then he thought about his toes and imagined them unfolding and relaxing one by one. After a while he moved on to the rest of his feet and then up into his ankles . . .

Ten minutes later he thought he was falling asleep at last, only for his eyes to open and the relaxation he felt to fade away. He sat up. Then he got up. He rubbed his eyes, stretched and went to get himself a drink from the kitchen. The light in there made him squint and his head started to pound again. He went back to his room and lit a cigarette, took three drags, felt sick and put it out. He downed his juice in one and went to get some more. This time he walked into the living room and turned on the telly. He sat and stared at the screen, flicked the channels and then checked

Teletext for football news, just like he always did. After he'd failed to read the screen through bleary eyes, he went back to flicking channels for another ten minutes. But none of it helped and he threw the remote at the wall and went back to his bedroom.

He watched the light on the CD player for about five minutes. He put in an Angie Stone CD, one of Della's, and turned it on. This time he knew it was wrong as soon as the music began. It sounded like it was playing at just slightly the wrong speed. He turned it off and got back into bed again, trying to get some sleep. It didn't work. He needed something to help. Anything. He decided that he'd get some sleeping tablets or something later in the day.

Then he remembered his mum had a stash of brandy in the kitchen. He got up, went back to the kitchen and pulled it out of the cupboard. He got a glass, poured himself a shot and downed it. For a few seconds waves of nausea overtook him and he fought back the urge to retch. But then his stomach calmed and he poured another, then another. The fourth shot he took back with him to his room.

He looked at the drugs, wanting another touch, even though he knew that another touch now would make sleep even less likely. He thought about how he'd slagged off junkies to Billy, called them weak, and yet here he was: addicted. Just like the weak people he used to despise. He wondered how he had fallen so far, so quickly. Thought about how the corded muscles in his arms and legs had begun to grow soft; about how hard he had worked at kick boxing to get fit and strong, only to fuck it all up. That first hit was just a laugh – that's how he'd seen it at the time. But the first one was followed by the second and then the third, until he couldn't close his eyes without the whisper returning and urging him to take more.

He lit a cigarette and thought about Della and Will and Ellie – about his best friend Billy – and he fought back the urge to punch himself in the forehead. He sat and rocked himself slowly, his mind full of faces and words and happier times, and he began to cry. It was all gone, the past. Gone down the drain, like in that song by Al Campbell that Nanny played all the time. Now he was part of a different crew, part of his family again – only not in the way he had always wanted to be. His family were part of the problem, something that he understood but could do nothing about.

And then he pushed the doubts and the memories to the back of his mind and picked up the wrap of cocaine. 'Fuck it,' he said to himself. He tapped out the powder onto a CD cover. Used the edge of his flick-knife to snort three little piles of shit which made his nose burn. He smoked his cigarette a bit, downed his shot, smoked some more and then put it out. He got into bed and pulled the covers over his head, closed his eyes and rode the rush, hoping that it would knock him out. Then he got up, smoked another fag and went back under the duvet . . .

In the bathroom the clock ticked its way past ten in the morning.

EIGHTEEN

My biological dad told me to stop by one of the bars he ran with his partner, Ronnie Maddix, when I called him the following morning. I told him I'd be there for eleven. He laughed.

'Only be you and the manager there, bwoi. Mek it twelve and I might just be on time,' he said. He sounded tired.

'Late night?' I asked.

'Is there any other kind?'

'Why don't you tell me where you are and I'll come to you?' I suggested.

'Nah, man – best we just meet at the bar,' he said quickly.

'You got summat to hide, Dad?' I teased.

'Just lemme get my sleep, man.'

'Later,' I told him, putting the phone down.

My mum was getting ready to leave for work

when I went into the kitchen. She looked at me in surprise.

'Who was that on the phone so early?' she asked. 'And what are you doin' up anyway – you feeling ill?'

I yawned and poured myself some juice. 'Couldn't sleep and that was Ellie,' I lied. 'Wants me to walk with her to school or some shit.'

'Foul-mouthed even in the morning,' she replied. 'I wish you wouldn't swear when you're talking to me.'

'Man, you sound like them teachers at school,' I told her.

I had grown up in an environment in which people swore all day long every day and it had rubbed off, I guess. I didn't tell my mum that though. She would only have felt guilty and blamed herself for it. Not that it was anyone's fault. It was just the way things were. Besides which, I'd used much worse language.

'I'm going to be late tonight, Billy, and Nanny reckons he's got to go see Patrick—'

'Tek Life?' I asked, intrigued.

'Yeah, him – so you'll have to get your dinner yourself. I've left you some money if you need it. It's in the living room.'

I was about to say thanks but she was already out of the door. Instead I wondered where my dog was. And, as if he could read my mind, Zeus padded in from the hall.

'Hey, dog breath,' I said, grabbing him by his big, fat head and giving him a rub.

He was so lazy he even moaned at that. Maybe he wasn't used to moving his head so quickly. I pushed him away and put the kettle on, hoping that coffee would take away the tiredness I was feeling. And I wondered what Nanny needed to see Tek Life about. I'd met him in the summer for the first time, and I knew that he was a part of Nanny's past, from before his conversion to Rastafarianism. Tek Life was a funny bloke, with a strange sense of what belonged to who. His real name was Patrick; the nickname had come from a sound system that he'd hung around with as a youngster – something to do with the way he danced, as far as I could remember. Whatever Nanny wanted with Patrick, it was definitely something connected to the night before. Patrick knew everything and everyone.

I was making myself a coffee when Nanny walked in and gave me the same surprised look as my mum.

'You get up early or yuh still haffe go a bed?' he asked with a smirk.

'Bit of both,' I replied, yawning.

'You need to relax 'bout everything from last

night, blood – me have it in hand,' he told me, smiling.

'Yeah, but I wanna do something too,' I admitted.

'Look after yuh family and yuh friends dem – don't worry 'bout the other t'ing,' he said again.

'Is that why you're meeting up with Tek Life?' I asked.

Nanny raised an eyebrow and looked at me for a moment. Then he grinned. 'Tek Life an' me have some business to deal wid,' he told me.

He grabbed a mug from the tree and got a herbal tea bag from its box, made himself a cup and left the kitchen.

My dad was yawning when I sat down opposite him in a city-centre bar. He had a fried-egg sandwich and a steaming mug of coffee in front of him.

'Easy, my yout',' he said, before biting into his food.

'Awright . . .'

He chewed and then called out to the barman to get me a coffee if I wanted one. The barman looked at me and I nodded.

'Black, no sugar,' I told him.

He gave me a thumbs-up and turned to the gleaming machine behind him. I watched my father eat and realized that he attacked his food with the same venom as I did – like the sandwich had done something to offend him. He finished it quickly and wiped his mouth on a serviette.

'So what can I do for you today?' he asked.

'You say that like seein' me is hard work,' I told him. 'Not bad for a man who didn't even bother for years—'

'Don't start that,' he replied. 'I'm here now, ain't I?'

'Whatever – you find anything out for me?'

He took a swig of coffee before replying. 'Three brothers – all dealin' – and yuh friend is helping them,' he told me.

'Shit—'

'Shit, brown, weed, pills – you name it, them man is selling it,' he said.

'All of it?' I was shocked.

'Nah – not all. Most of the rock is still with the usual people – although there's a load of Kosovans causing trouble for dem.'

I nodded. 'How do you know Jas is dealing for them anyway?' I asked.

He shrugged. 'How do I know anything? It don't matter who told me – that's what's happenin'. From what I hear yer man is doing the shit too—'

'Nah,' I protested. 'He might *just* be stupid enough to be dealin' but he ain't takin' it – I know him like he's my brother.'

Lynden looked away for a moment and something passed in his eyes.

'*What?*' I asked.

'Nuttin'. I'm tellin' you what I know, Billy. Not what I heard – what I *know*, you get me?'

'This just gets worse,' I replied, more to myself than to him.

He gave me a funny look. 'Is there something else, kid?'

I should have told him what was going on. No matter what kind of wanker he'd been to me and my mum, he was still my dad and he would have helped Nanny sort things out – I know he would. But instead I kept my mouth shut and thanked him for the information. It was *my* problem and I wanted to deal with it. After all, he hadn't been there when I needed him to teach me to ride a bike or read to me at night, and that was still a sore point with me. Besides which, if I changed my mind he was only a phone call away.

'Just mind who you talk to,' he told me. 'A load more dealers got picked up and there's a whisper goin' round 'bout man chatting other people's business. Yuh nuh want that t'ing to end up at your door.'

Too late for that, I said to myself.

'*Wha'?*' he asked.

'Nuttin' – thanks for the coffee, Dad. I've gotta go.'

'Where?'

'Work,' I lied.

'Doin' *what*, man? You know you can come work wit' me anytime yuh like,' he told me.

'I know that,' I replied. 'But I ain't interested.'

He shrugged as someone put a meaty hand on my shoulder.

'Billy the Kid. How's it *hangin'*, blood?'

It was Ronnie Maddix. I turned and smiled at him.

'Easy, Ronnie,' I said.

'All right, kiddo – how's yer mam?' he growled. He didn't really have any other tone of voice.

'Cool.'

'What about that dreadlocked bumboclaat?' he continued.

For a moment I nearly erupted, thinking that he was dissing Nanny, but then I realized he was just being himself. A knob.

'He's cool, Ronnie. Usual.'

Ronnie squeezed his massive frame in next to my dad and shouted at the barman.

'Oi, Shirley! Get us a coffee, will yer, an' get the kid whatever he likes.'

'I'm OK,' I told him. 'Gotta go—'

'But I only just got here,' he said.

'Still gotta go,' I repeated.

'Got some balls, your kid, Lynden,' he said.

'*Jah know*,' laughed my dad.

'Must get 'em off his mam — you ain't got 'em,' he grinned.

I shook my head, told Ronnie to get stuffed and left them to their morning. What was left of it. Outside, rain was falling and there was a cold wind blowing. I pulled up my hood and headed back to the ghetto, desperate to get hold of Jas if I could, and the rest of the crew. We had to do something to help him. His cousins had obviously led him the wrong way and we had to put it right. I had seen too many young lads go down the path that Jas was on, and not many of them came back the same.

NINETEEN

I saw the first poster as I entered the estate, on my way to the community centre to see Gary, the youth worker. I wanted to know if he had seen Jas, and to leave a message with him. Only I didn't get that far. At first I thought my eyes were playing tricks with my mind or someone had slipped me a pill, but the only drinks I'd had were with my dad and my other dad, and neither of them would have done it; and my eyes were working just fine. It was stuck to a boarded window, on one of the ground-floor flats, covering up a load of graffiti. I walked over and looked at it.

There was a picture on it. Of me. I was lying on what looked like concrete, with my eyes shut. It was a grainy image, as if it had been scanned by a regular person and not someone who knew what they were doing. Or like the kind of photo my old phone took. Beneath the picture in bright red numerals was a phone number. My old number. Instinctively I span round and checked if anyone was about, watching. Waiting. A few kids were hanging around in one of the stairwells in the opposite block and I could hear a baby screaming somewhere. The *mugging*, I thought. The lads who had attacked me had taken my photo with my own phone. I shook my head and turned back to the poster.

Above the photo, in block capitals, it read: WANTED DEAD OR *NOT* ALIVE FOR INFORMING. Then, between the photo and the phone number, was my name. Underneath this was smaller print which said, CALL THE NUMBER ABOVE TO TELL THIS GRASS THAT HE'S DEAD. Finally, in bright green letters, it said: REWARD.

I looked around again, hoping to catch someone in the act of putting another one up. My mouth had gone dry and my hands were sweating. Inside my head, my blood was beginning to boil. I tore at the poster, pulling a long strip off, screwed it up and threw it to the ground. Then I set off for my house, already dialling Will. I got as far as the next block before I saw three more posters. Something in my head exploded.

I rushed towards them and began to pull and scrape them off, only these were stuck fast, despite the rain. I looked around, frantically searching for something to use and spotted an empty bottle of lager. I picked it up and then smashed it against the concrete floor. I was left with a shard of glass and some cuts. I walked over to the first poster and began to use the glass to scrape it off. Once I'd defaced it enough, I moved on to the next and then the next. I threw the glass to the floor once I'd finished, swore and walked on.

As I rounded the far end of the estate into a row of terraced streets, just behind the community centre I saw even more posters. Someone had pasted every available surface with them: over the top of other posters advertising gigs and bands and new CDs. Over the windows of empty houses, on gates, even onto boards which were tied around the lampposts. I stood and stared at them in disbelief. I was in shock. Too shocked for about ten minutes to realize that the only safe place for me was my house: off the street and out of the way. I just stood where I was like a nutter who hadn't taken his pills for a while. Then I came to, pulled up my hood, tightened it around my face and set off for home at a sprint.

I went in round the back, via the alley, dodging past a smashed-up telly that had been dumped and a little Somalian kid, who smiled and showed me the toy in his hands, a rubber hammer.

Normally I would have stopped but I just went on through my gate and closed it behind me. Only when I got to the back door did I pull my hood down. I leaned forward and placed my hands on my knees, trying to take deep breaths. I slowly returned to normal, although my lungs were burning and I felt light headed. When I was feeling a little better, I found my key and tried the back door. It was already open . . .

Quickly, I went back into the yard and found a spade in the shed. I held it in front of me, my grip tight, and walked slowly back to the door. Nudging it open with the spade, I waited for a couple of seconds to see if anyone came at me. No one did. I inched my way inside. Everything seemed normal. There was no sign of a break-in and the kitchen was its usual tidy self. I walked slowly towards the kitchen door, opened it cautiously and looked down the hallway. Nothing. There was nothing wrong in the downstairs rooms either and when I eventually worked my way upstairs, nothing had been disturbed. One of the family must have forgotten to lock the back door. I thought back to the morning and knew that it hadn't been me. Still, I was relieved that I had been wrong to think that someone had broken in. Feeling only slightly better, I went back downstairs to the kitchen and found my mum's fags. I lit one and sat down at the table, trying to calm down. Something on the front of the local paper caught my eye – an article on the drug arrests – and I picked it up, nearly falling off my chair as I did so. Underneath the paper was my old mobile phone.

Nanny turned up around five in the afternoon, his brow furrowed and his eyes set hard, like they were cut from flint. He walked into the kitchen, where I was still sitting, and swore. In front of me my old mobile and my new one were full to bursting with unanswered calls and text messages. I knew that the answer machine in the hallway was the same because I hadn't bothered to answer a single call all afternoon. I had just sat where I was, thinking and smoking and trying not to panic.

'You seen 'em,' I asked.

'Me see dem,' he told me, his voice edged with steel.

'I'm fucked,' I said to him.

'Me an' Patrick drive to Nottingham fe go check one a we bredren an' when we return I man see nuff a dem *raasclaat* poster all over the place.'

'I tried to get rid of some, scrape 'em off,' I told him, 'but there was too many.'

He came over and put a hand on my shoulder. 'Don't worry yuhself, Billy. Patrick a gwan check fe some a dem man – find out wha' 'appen,' he said softly.

'What?' I asked, unsure what he meant. 'What men?'

'Some of de dealer dem – maybe check out Ronnie – see if him know what a gwan.'

'And then what?' I asked, not telling Nanny that I'd already been to see Lynden, although not about the whisper.

'Then we ago find out which man behind all dis and we a gwan set dem pon de right road,' he said.

'The right road?'

'Yeah,' he whispered. 'We ago mek dem see de light – Jah know.'

I picked up my old phone and held it out to him. 'This was here when I got in. The back door was open.'

Nanny swore in a way that I'd never heard him swear before. Then he threw the mobile phone at the wall. It cracked open and fell to the floor. He sat down and pulled out a small spliff from his shirt pocket and lit it.

'This is bad,' he said, as swirls of ganja smoke danced around his head like they had minds of their own.

'What we gonna do?' I asked, unsure of our next step.

'I dunno, Billy,' he replied quietly. 'Right dis secon' me nuh 'ave a fockin' clue.'

Everyone saw the posters. Ellie saw them on her way home from school with her brother. Her mum and dad were shopping and stopped on the way back outside the precinct off-licence to grab some beers. Next to a poster of two-for-the-price-of-one lagers they saw a picture of me lying out cold on the pavement. Will rang and told me they were all over his street, even pasted to the bins. And Della came over with a face like thunder, unable to understand why someone had it in for us so badly. Even my dad left me a message, telling me to get in touch straight away. The only person who didn't see them was my mum, who had been at a meeting out of town all day and didn't get back until around nine-thirty.

She breezed in, smiling as she saw Will, Ellie, Della, me and Nanny sitting around the kitchen table. A smile that disappeared when she saw our faces.

'What's wrong?' she asked us, the worry lines showing on her forehead.

'Sit down, Mum,' I replied. 'We're in trouble . . .'

TWENTY

We started by telling her about the mugging. Her face fell when I explained what had happened and she began to get angry. I told her that at the time I hadn't thought anything of it – it was just one of those things that happen. I told her that I'd asked Nanny to keep quiet over it because I didn't want to stress her out. She shook her head and asked me what I thought she was feeling now – after the event. I didn't know what to say. Instead I went on to tell her about the graffiti on the wall by the school and the way we had dealt with the kids who were picking on Ellie. All the way through she cursed and called us idiots – asking us why we hadn't told her or Sue or any of the other parents.

Then I said that I believed the attacks were linked to the whisper that was going around. I pulled out the note that had been left after the second attack and showed it to her.

'Why the *hell* didn't you show this to Lucy Elliot when she was here?' demanded my mum.

'Why do you *think*, Mum? Talking to coppers is what we're in trouble over – even though we ain't done it—'

'That has to be the stupidest piece of logic I've ever heard from you, Billy, and I've heard some shit. She's a *police* detective – it's her *job* to protect us,' she replied.

'I ain't talking shit,' I snapped. 'There's dealers getting hooked up by the Babylon all over town – bad men are getting turned over – and they're all blaming us. *Us!* These people don't play no *rules.*'

She glared at me, telling me that I had over-stepped the mark. That there was nothing I could tell her about 'bad men' that she hadn't found out for herself. She was right too, only that made me even angrier because she should have been the first one to realize that the police couldn't help people like us. Not where we lived. That was the way things were for the people society cared about. Not for us. The police didn't exist as anything good for ninety-five per cent of the people who lived where we did, and they had themselves to blame for it. They represented someone else.

'What about you?' she asked Nanny. 'I suppose you're going to tell me that the police are out of the question too?'

Nanny waited for a while before answering, and as he waited, I watched my mum's face calm visibly. Nanny understood her better than I did.

'What yuh want I to say? Right now, *right this minute*, man is looking for us to confirm dem lie by calling the police. We do that and whoever a plant dis lie gwan tell the dealers, "Yuh see it deh? Me done *tell* yuh dem bwoi a informer!"'

I saw the lack of understanding in Ellie's face so I repeated what Nanny had just said for her.

'Calling the police will make the people who did this happy because that's what they *want* us to do. So that they — whoever *they* are — can go to the dealers and say, "See? We told you they were the informers!" — it's what they want.'

Ellie mouthed 'Thank you' to me and continued to listen to the conversation. My mum was trying to tell Nanny that things had gone too far and that it was ridiculous for us to think that our neighbours and friends would point fingers at us over some stupid lies. But then I told her about the posters and how they had planned the mugging just to get my phone. She went as near to white as she can get.

'And when I got back today, they had come in the back door. They left my old phone for me — as a warning — it's over there on the side — what's left of it, anyway,' I added.

She got up and found some fags in her bag, lit one and sat back down. Without speaking, she looked at each one of us in turn before telling us that she needed to think. She got up and walked out of the kitchen. The mood was edgy so I thought I'd try to liven it up a bit.

'Zeus round at yours today?' I asked Ellie.

She looked at me sheepishly, like she needed permission to talk. 'No – I've not seen that smelly thing today.'

'He's probably in your bed again,' suggested Will, only I knew that he wasn't because I had checked the whole house for signs of intruders.

'Nah, he's probably here somewhere – asleep, no doubt,' I said.

Nanny got up without a word and left the room too. I watched him go, knowing that he was going to talk to my mum some more, waiting until he'd shut the door before speaking.

'There's something else too,' I told my friends.

'Man – what else could there be?' said Della, exasperated.

'You ain't gonna like it,' I warned her.

'Just tell us, Billy,' demanded Will.

'I went to see my dad earlier – Lynden. He told me that Jas is dealing drugs with his cousins – and taking them too.'

There was silence. Will looked at the ceiling,

then the floor. Ellie looked at Della and Della looked at me.

'You *what*?' she asked.

'That's what he heard,' I told her. 'Why would he make it up?'

'But I would *know*,' she said, only quietly.

'Would you *really*?' I asked. 'How many times have you *seen* him recently?'

Della looked away and then back again. 'That's not fair,' she said.

'I'm sorry – I didn't mean to snap at you. It's just that he could be doing *anything* and *none* of us would know.'

'Ain't like he's one of us no more anyhow,' said Will with a shrug.

I hadn't openly said as much but I agreed with Will. Jas had become a stranger. He had gone from being a friend we could have trusted with our lives to someone who wouldn't even reply to one out of every hundred phone calls or messages. I thought about how our friendship, mine and his, had taken ten years to build but just over eight months to take apart. It was an upsetting thought.

'But he's still one of *us*,' insisted Ellie. 'He's *still* Della's boyfriend—'

Della shook her head. 'Not if he's doin' that shit, he ain't,' she told us.

'What you gonna say to him?' I asked.

'I dunno – but that bwoi is getting forty-eight hours from now to get in touch. Otherwise he's dust and I don't care what he says. I'm gonna shut the door in his face for good.'

She found her phone and started to type a message. After she'd sent it she threw her phone on the table.

'There,' she said, 'I've done it – man's got two days.'

Her eyes told me that this time she wasn't joking. Della's biological mother had been a heroin addict and she hated hard drugs with a passion that was sometimes like a fire in her heart. It was a central part of what made her tick.

'I swear,' she added, after a moment, 'if he's been off his head when he's been with me – ain't no one alive can save his face from me.'

She sat for a moment or two longer, until suddenly she got up and ran out of the kitchen, crying. I heard her going up the stairs and knew she was heading to my room. I let her go and made Ellie stay too.

'She needs to be on her own, Baby.'

'But I just want to make sure that she's all right,' said a tearful Ellie.

'It's OK,' I said, getting up to give her a hug.

'No it's not,' cried Ellie. 'Everything is falling apart and we can't do anything to stop it.'

TWENTY-ONE

Ever since Nanny rescued me and my mum from a life in the tower blocks and no future, he's been able to make us see things his way. He doesn't bully people in a discussion the way some people do. He'll sit and listen, take things in, make comments and then reason with you. And most of the time he knows what he's talking about. I don't know what he said to my mum, but the next morning she told me she was going to have to trust that Nanny knew what to do.

'He has got a point,' she said. 'People round here don't always use the facts to make a judgement.'

'I know,' I replied.

'And if anyone can find out who's behind all this and put it right – it's Nanny's mates,' she added.

'I just wish we knew who it was now,' I told her. 'It's so frustrating.'

'Well, he's gone out with Patrick to talk to a few people so we'll see what he comes up with. In the meantime, even though I'm not totally happy about not calling the police, we'll just have to wear it.'

I smiled at her although I was still angry at what had happened to me – not just the mugging but the posters too. It was like I had some kind of invisible enemy. I was stuck in the house and I didn't even have Zeus to mess around with. No one had seen him since the night before, although we weren't worried about him. Zeus was a temperamental dog and sometimes he'd just go off somewhere. I rang Ellie and told her to come over and keep me company. She was out with her mum and promised to turn up later in the day. Then I went and watched Saturday morning telly for a bit.

About three in the afternoon I turned on the radio and listened to the football as, outside, big drops of rain began to fall from the slate-grey sky. What light there was disappeared and the room was suddenly dark and cold. I switched a side lamp on and went back to the commentary. Something was nagging at my brain. I just couldn't put my finger on what it was. I went into the kitchen to get a cup of coffee, returning just in time to hear that my beloved Liverpool were a goal down to

Arsenal. I swore, kicked the sofa and turned the radio off. Then I returned to the kitchen and found a cigarette. I opened the back door and stood just inside it, watching the rain hammer down in the yard. Opposite the back of our house, on the other side of the alley, was another row of terraced houses and I spent my cigarette watching the windows for signs of life. There weren't any – not even from the house directly opposite ours, where a group of students lived.

I flicked my fag at the wall that divided my house from Ellie's and shut the door on the downpour. I searched my brain for something to do. I didn't want to listen to the football just in case I was a bad omen for my team and there was nothing on telly. The Internet was an option but I couldn't be arsed to go upstairs. Instead I went down into the cellar, which was Nanny's little den. My mum had had it converted a few years back so that you could stand up in it. The walls were lined with soundproofing and all Nanny's old vinyl was down there, along with his huge hi-fi system, complete with giant speaker boxes that made the house shake when you turned them up. I switched on his system, knowing that he wouldn't mind and searched the racks and racks of records, pulling some of them out. All of them – apart from maybe fifty or so – were old-time reggae from the seventies and eighties, with a load of sixties Ska thrown in as well.

I pulled out one of my favourites from childhood, a dub by the Wailing Souls called *Bredda Gravalicious*, and put it on. The bass on the amplifier was turned all the way down, and on his mixer, which sat between two Vestax turntables, the kill switch, which took the bass notes in and out of the mix, was turned off too. Letting the record begin, just like I had seen Nanny do for years, I turned the bass up to half way on the amp, waited for the bass line on the record to go through four bars and then dropped it in by flicking the kill switch on the mixer. The boom was enough to make the walls vibrate and I pulled up Nanny's swivel chair and sat back, letting the slow, hypnotic rhythm take over my mind and my heartbeat.

When the record finished, I lifted the needle and started it over again, pretending in my head that I was running the sound system that I saw at carnival every year. They were called Aba-Shanti-I and Nanny knew them from when he used to run his own sound. Aba-Shanti-I was the loudest sound system I had ever heard and the music they played, just like the dub I was playing, took over the beating of your heart until you became almost wrapped up in the mix and the music — like you'd dived into a pool of cotton wool. I spent the rest of the afternoon pulling out tunes that I remembered from my childhood and playing them over and over again. Bass heavy, conscious tunes by Black Uhuru, Dennis Brown, Augustus Pablo and the Twinkle Brothers. Somewhere in there I got so lost with the music and thinking about what was happening to me and my friends that I didn't even hear or see Ellie come down the stairs around six. I only realized she was there when she put her hand on my shoulder and made me jump.

'Bloody hell!' I shouted.

'Calm down, you old man,' she said with a grin.

'What?' I asked, turning down the music.

'I'm not surprised you didn't hear me – what is this rubbish anyway?' she asked.

'This isn't rubbish, young lady. If it wasn't for this music there'd be no hip-hop, house music, garage – none of it. This is where it all started,' I told her.

'Don't care,' she replied. 'So have you got me anything yet?'

I looked at her and for a second or two wondered what she was on about, but then the nagging feeling in my brain told me. Ellie was going to be fifteen the following Tuesday. I tried not to let my face betray that I'd forgotten.

'*Yeah* – course I have,' I told her. 'Got it *ages* ago.'

'So what is it then?' she asked excitedly.

'Not telling you – it's a surprise—'

'But I don't *like* surprises,' she told me. 'I like to know what I'm getting so that I can *pretend* to be surprised or work on my "oh it's lovely" act – just in case it's horrible.'

'You're supposed to be grateful to even *get* a present – not slag them off when you do,' I said, shaking my head.

'But that's just stupid,' she argued. 'Who does that?'

'Not you, obviously.'

'You're such an old man – I'm not sure I want to be your friend.'

She must have seen the look on my face, even though I tried to hide it. The thought – even as a joke – of losing another close friend made me frown. She leaned over and gave me a kiss. 'I'm only joking, you pensioner,' she said. 'You've been thinking about Jas, haven't you?'

I nodded. 'None of this makes any sense, Ellie. The whisper is one thing, but Jas doin' drugs? How can someone change so much in such a short space of time?' I asked her.

'I don't know,' she admitted. 'It's so sad.'

'Only eight months ago – when we had that trouble – we was all the best of friends and now I don't even know who he is.'

'Just think what Della's going through,' said Ellie.

I just shook my head.

'Don't worry, though – I'm always going to be your friend.'

I smiled at her. 'I hope so, Ellie.'

She looked at me with an intensity in her eyes that I only saw now and then, usually when she was feeling emotional. I thought she was going to cry but she caught herself and looked away.

'Besides,' she mumbled, going red, 'I'm your link to youth, old man. You'd be lost without me.'

'You ain't that much younger than me,' I said.

'But young enough so that you won't—' she began before stopping and picking up a record sleeve.

'I won't what?' I asked.

She looked at the sleeve for a moment before replying. 'Won't stop treating me like a kid.'

'OK – from Tuesday I'll start treating you like an adult – I promise.'

She looked at me, grinned and told me that she was going to hold me to that. I told her she could.

'We'll see,' she said with a little wink.

We got a pizza around eight in the evening and ate it as we watched an old Coen brothers film on DVD. My mum came in as the film started and stole some of my food, despite having complained about its saturated fat content when I'd ordered it. Then she sat between me and Ellie and made comments about the film all the way through. Della rang at a really good bit just to tell me she wasn't coming round: Sue had family over. And at the most exciting point I got a text from Will to say that he was going out with his brother and would catch up with me the following day. Finally we finished watching the film and my mum farted really loud. It was one of those nights.

I realized that Nanny wasn't back and my mum told me that he'd called to say he was going to be late. I wondered what he'd found out, if anything, before asking Ellie what she wanted to do next.

'Dunno.' She shrugged. 'I don't want to go home and it's not a school night so you can't play at being my dad for a change.'

'We could go and listen to some more music,' I suggested, but she crinkled up her nose.

'I'd quite like to watch another of those Coen brothers movies,' she said.

'A girl after my own heart,' my mum told me. 'I'm up for it—'

'Who asked you – old fart?' I said.

My mum looked at Ellie, shook her head and then picked up a leftover slice of pizza. As she went to eat it, I leaned forward to grab the remote control and she slapped the back of my neck with the pizza slice.

'Urrrgh!' I shouted, as my mum and Ellie burst into laughter.

They were still laughing when I returned from the bathroom having cleaned myself up. 'Witches!'

'Don't speak to your mum like that,' said Ellie.

'Yeah,' added my mum. 'Thanks, Ellie.'

'And help yourself to pizza,' continued Ellie, with a broad grin. 'I don't want any more – you know what they say – a moment on the lips, a lifetime on the—'

'Neck?' suggested my mum, before they started laughing all over again.

I grabbed my mum's copy of *The Big Lebowski* and stuck it into the machine, muttering under my breath.

TWENTY-TWO

I woke up at the sound of the back door opening and realized that I had fallen asleep on the sofa. Not alone either. Ellie was curled up with me and had her head on my chest. For a moment I failed to register what was going on but then I got up slowly, hoping that Ellie wouldn't wake up. She didn't. I wondered when we had fallen asleep and why my mum had left us where we were – but not for long. I realized that it had to be Nanny at the back door and I wanted to know what he had found out. I shut the living-room door quietly and went into the kitchen.

Nanny was sitting at the table with a spliff on, his eyes set. I walked in and sat down opposite him.

'Hey,' I said.

He nodded and took a long drag on his spliff, waited for about thirty seconds and then let the smoke out slowly so that it floated in clouds around his head.

'You OK?' I asked.

He shrugged. 'I could lie to you, Billy, and say yes I'm fine but I'm not.'

I raised my eyebrows and frowned. 'What's up, Nanny.'

'People,' he told me. 'Chattin' fuckery.'

'What?'

He took another long drag before he spoke. 'Me an' Patrick went to talk to some man – find out 'bout dis problem – an' man and man convince dat I man a grass up all a de yout' dem wha' get arrest recently—'

'Huh?'

'We chat to everyone – some a dem man know me from me was a yout' – an' all a dem believe say a me de informer.'

'But the posters – they were about *me*,' I said.

'Is all the same t'ing, Billy. Dem tell me seh I must leave town less I man end up dead—'

'But—' I began.

Nanny shook his head. He was angry. 'Me nuh know who a chat all a these lie but dem doin' a good job,' he said flatly.

I gulped down air, aware that what Nanny was telling me meant trouble for all of us.

'From when dem man a chat 'bout me so – me can't stay round yah.'

'You mean you're going to leave? You can't,' I said.

'Wha' yuh want I fe do? Me can't stay here – is *me* dem pointing at, Billy. Even me own idren dem think seh me a informer.'

He took another long drag, and as he expelled the smoke my mum came into the kitchen. As soon as she saw Nanny's face she knew that something was wrong.

'What's up?' she asked him.

He told her what he had told me. The dealers and the bad men all over the area were convinced that it was Nanny who was informing the police. Even his old friends were whispering about him, pointing fingers, and everything that had happened with me was just a part of that.

'Someone a play with us,' he told her, 'and them playing the game well . . . And we nuh have a raasclaat clue who it is.'

'Is there any way to find out?' I asked.

He shrugged again. 'Patrick ago mek some enquiry and I man did speak to a few of me idren, but until we can prove it wasn't me t'ings gwan be tough.'

My mum's face fell. 'How tough?' she asked.

'Big man getting sent down. Nuff money dem

losin' – and all dem care about is the money. If dem t'ink seh I man in their way . . . Well, yuh know what them will do.'

He took a final pull on his spliff and stubbed the roach out in the ashtray just as my mum lit a fag. Her hand was shaking as she did it and I knew why. We were in real danger. The people that Nanny was talking about weren't like the criminals that you saw on TV. They were real, with real guns and real knives. If they thought that Nanny was fucking up their business, cutting their profits, they wouldn't hesitate to take him out, and use his family to get to him. They would kill him if that's what it took. It was no joke either – it had happened in the past. One man had been found with his tongue cut out and another, an illegal immigrant from Jamaica, who had tried to take over someone else's streets, had survived a shooting minus most of the left side of his face, which had been blown off with a sawn-off shotgun. The men Nanny was talking about took no prisoners, made thousands of pounds each week, and wouldn't let anyone get in the way of that.

'What are we going to do?' asked my mum.

'I don't know,' said Nanny. 'But I'm gonna go stay with some friends for a few days until we can sort it out. Patrick a gwan start a rumour dat me done leave town – jus' to find some time. It's too dangerous to stay. I'm gonna put you in danger too an' me nuh want that.'

'But where can you go?' she asked. 'And what about us?'

'I man ago stay with my bredren from Shanti sound – just for a few days – and until then Tek Life gwan tek care of you all.'

'He's going to stay *here*?' I asked.

'Is the only way, Billy. You know it mek sense. Them man deh wan get to me an' dem might jus' be stupid enough to come after mi family too. I jus' can't allow dat, seen?'

'But we can just call the police,' insisted my mum.

Nanny shook his head slowly. 'Even if Babylon protect we until dem catch half of the dealer, yuh t'ink dem man ago forget?'

He was right too. The police would be able to sort out our immediate problems but what would happen when they went on to their next case? The dealers and their friends would still be out there and we would be labelled for life, always having to watch out for them. And they wouldn't forget. It didn't work that way. Even if they waited a year, they would eventually come, and when they did it would be like nothing we had ever experienced before. No, the police were the worst people to turn to. The only people who could help us were the ones who understood our enemies and could set them straight. And the only way to do that was to find out who was setting us, and them, up.

'I'm gonna call Lynden,' I said.

My mum gave me a sharp look and then swore.

'Hol' on a minute, Rita,' said Nanny. 'Me know dat yuh and him have history but Billy is right – we need dem man to help us now.'

'Ronnie too,' I added. 'It's the only way. Between them two and Patrick we'll find out who's doing this to us.'

My mum did not look happy.

'Rita – come on, man. Yuh know is dem man we mus' call on fe straighten t'ings out.'

'But—' she began.

'When yuh have a fire yuh call de fire brigade, nuh true? We have a fire, Rita, and we can't put it out on we own.'

My mum's shoulders sagged and she looked sad. I think she was beginning to realize that we didn't have a choice. Lynden and Ronnie were our aces – people who our enemies couldn't push around and who'd back us up. Along with Patrick they were our only chance.

'I'll call him in the morning,' I told them.

'Call him now,' said Nanny. 'He'll be up and about – tell him seh we need to see him right now.'

'I don't believe this,' said my mum.

'Yuh an' me both, Rita,' Nanny told her.

I grabbed my phone and dialled Lynden's number.

I was outside having a fag an hour later, waiting for my dad to come round, when I heard Zeus whimpering at the gate to the alley. I wondered how he had managed to get out until I remembered that Nanny had come in that way. I hadn't seen Zeus for a few days. I opened the back gate, hoping that he hadn't been rolling around in mud or anything. What I saw when I opened the gate made me drop my fag.

Zeus was lying on his side in a pool of blood. Around his midriff was a plastic bag, tied with a length of rope. I knelt down slowly and put my hand on his head. He whimpered and then was silent. I untied the rope and removed the plastic bag, There was something inside. I opened the bag, getting blood on my hands, and saw the envelope. I opened it and read the letter. All it said was '*Nanny is a dead man*'. I dropped the letter, looked at Zeus and then turned away with tears in my eyes.

TWENTY-THREE

Three in the morning and Jas was feeling the high. Dee lined up a next smoke of rock but Jas shook his head as 50 Cent tore out the speakers in the hired Audi A3. They were parked up across the road from a block of flats on the Whitelaw Estate, waiting for Divy to return from some flat or other where he had a woman. Jas pressed a button on the stereo and the next CD kicked in. This time it was Makiavelli. He didn't want to listen to that one either. He pressed the button again and started some grimy garage compilation, heavy bass and hardcore, brain-deadening beats. The bass line took some of the edge off and he accepted the pipe from his cousin, lit it, inhaled and took another trip out of his mind.

Ten minutes later Divy came out of the building, walking past a gang of youths who, if they had been rich, would have been at home in bed by midnight. Thirteen-year-olds on the prowl, looking for people to mash up just for the hell of it. Bored and high on home-grown or glue. Or both. Divy said something to one of the lads, smiled and then came over to the car. Jas got out and let Divy get in the back, noticing the blood on his T-shirt.

'Wha' dat?' he asked, his head still predominantly somewhere else.

'Nuttin',' grinned Divy. 'Just some knobhead I had to get rough with – talkin' 'bout he ain't got my money.'

'Too right,' agreed Dee. 'You get high you gotta pay for the pie—'

'You what?' laughed Divy. 'You just made that up, you rocked-out mofo.'

'Yeah, man,' agreed Dee, looking out of the window.

'Where we goin' now?' asked Divy.

'Lap-dance place over the west end – my uncle owns it. Freebies, man,' laughed Dee, starting the car up and burning tyre rubber.

'Ease up,' said Jas. 'You'll get us pulled—'

'Raas dat!' shouted Dee, his voice manic.

Six in the morning and Jas lay in his bed, staring at the ceiling, after reading a text from Della. He wondered whether she was awake and thought about calling her, but his head was gone and he needed to sleep, not get stressed by his girlfriend. He sat up and wondered where his mum was. Working the late shift probably, he said to himself. He reached down to the floor beside the bed and picked up his jeans. In one of the pockets was a little wrap of brown, Jas's short cut to sleep. He smoked it just like Dee had shown him, just a touch. Just enough to get rid of the cold, metallic feeling in his head and the burning pain in his sinuses. The hit took a moment or two but then he started to feel warm and his toes relaxed. He thought about the technique he'd seen on that telly programme, lay back and chuckled to himself. Sleep wouldn't be long in coming . . .

TWENTY-FOUR

My dad turned up at around ten in the morning. He stank of stale weed smoke and booze and his eyes were red. I opened the door and walked him into the kitchen. My mum had taken Zeus to a twenty-four-hour vet. He had been out cold when she left with him, a deep gash in his side that looked like it had been cut with a knife. I was anxious to hear about him. I hadn't been back to sleep either and had left Ellie where she was. She was still snoring away.

'Where's yer mum?' asked Lynden, sitting down at the table.

'You want a coffee?' I said with a yawn, ignoring his question.

He nodded. 'Black. Strong,' he replied, before asking after my mum again.

'Different woman to the one you knew,' I told him, with just a hint of pride.

'Different everything now, Billy.'

'Why did you leave?'

I shocked even myself with my question. I hadn't wanted to ask it and I couldn't work out why I had. Sometimes when you're tired things slip under the fence between your conscious and subconscious without your control. At least that's what I put it down to afterwards. Lynden glanced at me and then looked away again.

'This ain't the right time for that conversation,' he said to me.

'There ain't no right or wrong time,' I replied. 'It just is.'

He shook his head. 'It nah go so, kid. I'll tell you soon, I promise. It's just that there's more to it than you think and I'm a bit more worried about this mess you're all in at the moment.'

I shrugged and made him a cup of coffee, which I set down in front of him.

'So?' he asked.

'So *what*?'

He looked away again. 'Where's No-Risk?'

I raised my eyebrows. '*Who?*'

'I'm sorry – Nanny,' he said, grinning.

'Why'd you call him No-Risk?' I asked.

'You'll have to ask him,' replied my dad. 'Where is he anyway?'

I let it go and told Lynden that Nanny had left

with Tek Life during the night. I didn't tell him where Nanny had gone though. Regardless of him being my blood, the fewer people knew where Nanny was, the better.

'Tek Life should be back around lunch,' I said.

He shook his head and let out a deep sigh. 'What the fuck is going on anyway?' he asked.

'Like you don't know,' I replied.

He took a swig of coffee and lit a fag. 'You better *leave* the lip, Billy,' he said sternly, 'and start at the beginning. I'm taking a big risk for you and I wanna know why I'm having to do it.'

In my head I swore but I began to tell him anyway.

My mum rang around half-eleven, telling me that Zeus would be OK but that he had needed stitches in a deep wound. The vet had asked her, suspiciously, about what had happened. She told me that she had made up a story about Zeus cutting himself on a broken window panel in a door, as he tried to get out. The vet had accepted her story but still looked worried.

'He might end up calling the police or the RSPCA,' she said.

'Nah – he sounds like he fell for it,' I told her.

'Who does that to a *dog*?' she whispered.

'I told you, Mum. These people ain't playin'—'

'I know that, Billy,' she said, 'but we should still tell Lucy Elliot—'

'*Mum.*'

'OK, OK. I'll let it go for now but if anything else happens I'm straight on the phone.'

'Yeah,' I said, dismissing what she said.

'Is he there yet?' she asked, changing the subject.

'Lynden? Yeah, he's in the kitchen.'

'Call me when he leaves,' she told me.

'Why?'

'So I can come home,' she replied. 'I don't wanna see him – not in the mood I'm in.'

I told her that I'd call her later and put the phone down. Back in the kitchen, my dad was yawning again.

'If you're tired,' I told him, 'you can go home to bed.'

He shook his head. 'Not until Tek Life gets here,' he replied.

I shrugged. 'So – what do you think?'

'About the problem you got? It's a hard one, kid. If the dealers think that you and Nanny are grassing them up – it's gonna be hard to convince them otherwise.'

'But someone's setting us up,' I told him.

'How do you know for sure?'

I looked at him like he was mad. 'Have you

listened to *anything* I told you? The posters, the attacks on the house – Zeus – what more do you *need*?'

'And you want me and Ronnie to find out who this person is?' he asked.

'Yeah – someone has to know.'

He sighed. 'But even if we find whoever it is, it might be too late anyway. The whisper is out there, Billy. Everyone thinks that it's you and Nanny – how we gonna change *that*?'

I thought about it for a minute before replying. 'We find out who it is and give them to the dealers,' I said angrily.

'*What?* They'll only deny they did it,' he said. 'You think this is some film, son? People are losing money – even me and Ronnie.'

'*What?*'

'Two of our associates got nicked in the last raid – just after they'd picked up a load of stuff.'

I looked at him in horror. 'Is that what you care about – *money*? Because if it is you can get lost right *now*,' I snapped.

'No, Billy – I'm here for *you*. Because you *asked* me to be here. You're my *son*, regardless of whatever else has happened, and if you think I'm gonna let someone hurt you – you're *mad*.'

I calmed down immediately. I'd never heard him say anything like that. It felt good to hear him tell me that I meant something to him. All the way through my childhood that was all I had ever wanted. Just to know that he cared – even if he wasn't around. I felt a wave of emotion escape down my spine.

'I'm sorry,' I said to him.

'There's loads of stuff we need to talk about, Billy, and we will, after all of this is sorted out, but right now we need to concentrate on this. OK?'

I nodded.

'Good,' he said. 'I'm gonna call Ronnie and get him to ask around – and then I'm going home to bed 'cos I'm knackered but I'll be back later.'

'Mum might not like it,' I admitted.

'Never mind that – this is more important. Right, have you got a number for Tek Life? I wanna know where he is.'

I pulled out my phone and gave it to him. He began to scroll through the address book, as I stood up and cleared away the coffee mugs, hoping that he would be able to help us. He was right though – it wouldn't be easy – but just the fact that he was on our side would help. The other people involved in street business were more likely to listen to one of their own. Especially if it was Ronnie Maddix, a man who hated the police in the same way that some people hate wasps.

Ellie left around two in the afternoon, upset that I'd let her sleep for so long and just a little embarrassed when she realized that we had spent part of the night together. She mumbled something about calling me later and left through the back door, her hair all over the place and sleep in her eyes. My mum had returned an hour before and was having a chat with Tek Life. She refused to use his street name – she called him Patrick. I sat and listened to one of Nanny's basement tapes, before putting a Garnett Silk CD on.

Will and Della turned up around four o'clock, looking cold.

'What's up with you two?' I asked, as I let them in.

'We've been all over the place,' Della told me, 'removing them stupid posters—'

'*Really?*' I asked.

'Yeah really,' Will said. 'Scraping them off in the rain or painting over them.'

He showed me his jeans, which had paint stains on them. 'You think I wear clothes like this for fun?' he asked.

'Where'd you get the paint?' I asked him.

'He nicked it from work,' said Della. 'Mek us a cup of tea, Billy. I'm freezing my tits off.'

'Sit down,' I said to them, feeling grateful and

relieved that they had bothered to go out in the rain to get rid of the posters.

'Seen that stupid bwoi again,' Della told me.

'Who?'

'That Tyrone – you know, the kid who don't like you?'

'Oh right. He give you any shit?' I asked.

'Nah,' said Will, shaking his head. 'He came up and asked us what we was doing and I told him. He looked shocked, mumbled something and walked off.'

A light went on in my head. 'He's one of them,' I said quietly.

'Nah – he can't be,' said Della.

'Why not?' I asked her. 'Why would he go all funny when you spoke to him. Look all shocked and that?'

'Maybe . . .' said Will.

'Well, he's going on the "man we gotta talk to" list. I'm gonna get Lynden to talk to him.'

Both of them looked at me in surprise.

'Lynden?' asked Will.

'Your old man? The *fit* one?' added Della.

'Yeah,' I told them, realizing that they needed to be brought up to speed. 'It's been a long night . . .'

PHONE CALL

'You done the posters?'

'Yeah, B. Everyone's talking about them now.'

'Nice. What about the other thing?'

'Tomorrow night — about eleven.'

'You sure, Divy?'

'Yeah — they told me themselves. The older one is going to do the deal — Malk.'

'Can you get the information to the police before then?'

'No problem, B. I'm gonna drop them a call straight after we've talked.'

'And what about the other brothers?'

'Once the older one is nicked, they'll go mad. That's when I'll tell 'em about Nanny and the rest.'

'And they'll believe you?'

'Thanks to the posters, yeah. You should work for MI5 or some shit, Busta. Talk about planning to the max.'

'Ain't a lot else to do in here, Divy.'

'I suppose . . .'

'Now we'll see who's the badman — that dutty dread ain't gonna know what's hit him.'

'I heard a rumour that he's done a runner.'

'He'll be back soon enough — once his fucked-up family get done.'

'You remember what you said about us bein' partners when you get out?'

'Yeah, I done that deal with the coppers — ain't that long left in here — twelve months tops. You keep on getting rid of the competition meantime, by the time I'm out there won't be no one left to touch us.'

'Like I said, man, planned to the max.'

'Just mek sure things go smoothly. And what about Jas?'

'Don't worry 'bout him — he gets in the way, I'll deal with it.'

'Cool — I'm gonna send you a VO soon — sort out the future, bro, face to face.'

'I'll look forward to it, B. Later . . .'

'Later, Divy.'

TWENTY-FIVE

Tyrone waited for Divy to walk off before coming out of his hiding place. Divy had been standing at the bottom of a stairwell in one of the tower blocks, talking on the phone to someone called Busta. He obviously didn't hear or see Tyrone as he left his aunt's flat. Didn't realize that he was hiding, three flights up, listening. Tyrone watched Divy head across the square in front of the tower block and disappear towards the main road. He waited a few moments, pulled up his hood to keep the rain off his head and stepped outside.

He went looking for the people Divy was setting up. The two he had seen earlier, getting rid of the posters that were all over the place, that everyone was chatting about. He felt sick, realizing that he had been part of it all, getting innocent people into trouble when the real informer was Divy. Not that he had any reason to help that

Billy. The bwoi was a dickhead. But he didn't want to get involved in what Divy was doing either, and he didn't want to get a reputation around here. He'd only moved to the area recently and he didn't want to rock the boat. Divy would get found out soon enough – it was bound to happen, and Tyrone didn't want to be talked about as one of his crew. That would get him into a whole heap of bother – not least with his dad, who was known and wouldn't like the hassle of having a son who was labelled an informer. So he went looking for the big lad, Will.

He walked down to the community centre, past loads of the posters which had been painted over or scraped off. He was hoping that Will and the girl he had been with were still around. He didn't know what he was going to say to them if he found them but he knew he had to say something. People knew that he was one of Divy's crew already. Everyone around the community centre and outside school had seen them chatting. And there was Sean too, who had introduced Tyrone to Divy in the first place. He'd helped Sean to mug Billy for his phone, all to help a grass. The more he thought about it, the worse he felt.

After the community centre he went by the precinct and then round onto the main road, where he saw Divy again, sitting in a car with two

Asian lads. He walked past on the opposite side of the road, his head down, so that he wouldn't be spotted. Quickly he stepped up a side street and walked on. He got as far as place where he'd mugged Billy and stopped. Billy lived down the end of the road, the house they'd been paid to mash up a few times. He stood and watched it for a minute. Then the strangest thing happened. A car pulled up and his dad got out of it, knocked on Billy's door and spoke to some woman for a bit. They looked like they were arguing about something and then his dad turned and left. Tyrone ducked behind a big bin as his dad looked his way, hoping that he hadn't been seen. He waited for him to leave and then turned and walked back the way he had come. His dad knew someone at Billy's house. The Asian woman at the door. He wondered what they had in common, his dad and the woman. And he wondered what that meant about his dad and Billy. If they knew each other, Tyrone would get into even more shit if he got found out.

He walked over the main road, deciding to leave things for the moment. If things got on top, he'd speak to his dad, but not before that. There was no point getting himself in trouble just yet. It could wait. As he rounded his own street corner he saw that his dad had turned up; he walked slowly up the two flights of the low-rise block and opened the door to the flat where he lived with his mum. His dad was lying on the sofa watching Man Utd playing Newcastle.

'Easy, Tee,' said his dad warmly.

'Hi, Dad.'

'Do me a favour, will you?' asked his dad.

'Yeah?'

'Get me a beer will yer – I'm knackered.'

Tyrone headed into the kitchen, still trying to work out what his dad had in common with Billy and his family.

TWENTY-SIX

Nanny rang the following afternoon. I was lying on the sofa, bored out of my mind and trying to decide whether I should chance a visit to the off-licence to get some fags. He sounded kind of sad and didn't say much apart from telling me that he was fine and that he was going to a dance with Aba-Shanti-I sound the following night in Brixton. I told him about Lynden coming round and went through what was happening.

'T'ings should cool off whilst I'm gone,' he told me.

'Things are already pretty quiet,' I replied. 'No one has put up any more posters and the house hasn't been targeted again.'

'Jus' keep on your toes, Billy. They didn't go to this much trouble jus' fe let it go.'

'I know,' I told him. 'Tek Life is here anyway – he's sleeping – but he's around.'

Nanny let out a chuckle. 'Dat bwoi too lazy,' he said.

'Lynden called you No-Risk yesterday,' I told him. 'What did he mean?'

'Raas – me nuh hear dat name fe time,' he replied.

'Yeah – but what does it mean?'

'Back when I was younger – before me find Rastafari I man did nuff bad t'ings . . . I used to be the most reliable driver fe getaway—'

'You mean a getaway as in robberies?'

'Yeah, man,' he admitted. 'Any man could ask me fe mi skills as long as dem pay de right money – an' dem neveh have no risk involve cah I man was the don.'

'Really?'

'Yeah man – no one ever catch me.'

I laughed. 'Apart from when you went to prison.'

I knew he was smiling on the other end of the line as he spoke.

'Yeah – apart from dat,' he said. 'So, because my slave name was Norris dem start call me No-Risk.'

Nanny called his pre-Rasta name his slave name because he believed that society kept people in mental chains, slaving away to earn money for the rich people up at the top and kept happy by an addiction to buying cars and houses and other material things. *If you think you are happy*, he'd say, *you won't see the* shitstem *that you live in and so you won't revolt against it. Mental chains. Your enemy is the man next door who has the things you want when really both you and your neighbour should be taking your rightful due from the liars and* politricksters *who ran things.* It was part of his philosophy and I kind of believed it too.

He rang off, saying that he'd call to speak to Ellie the next day because it was her birthday. I went back into the living room, still wondering whether I should venture out or not. In the end Tek Life came downstairs and told me that he'd take me out in his car, with its ear-splitting sound system and blacked-out windows. I jumped at the chance to get out: I pulled on a hooded top and grabbed my phone and my cash.

Tek Life took the main road and drove across the iron bridge onto the ring road, jumping a red light as he fiddled with his stereo and tried to light a spliff at the same time. I checked my belt just to be safe and settled back. Dread reggae music began to pulse through the speakers, warning the world that Armageddon was on its way and that the people should repent before their sins took them to hell. Just the sort of light-hearted subject that would lift my mood. Over the top of a rumbling, continuous bass line he told me that he had to pick up a 't'ing' on the other side of the city.

'You want one a my cigarette – help yourself but open the window,' he told me. 'Me nuh like de smoke, man.'

I was about to say that his spliff had filled the car with smoke anyway and what was the difference, but I stopped myself. Instead I heard the opening to a tune called *Going the Wrong Way* by Al Campbell and took the spliff that Patrick offered me, drawing hard and then letting the sweet feeling take over. Patrick laughed as he swerved across two lanes of traffic and jumped another red light, heading up over a flyover and down the other side like he was flying a plane rather than driving a car. He turned left at the bottom and into an estate that had been notorious years earlier for being full of racists. The ethnic mix had changed though, and now it was just like where we lived, only on the edge of the city, separated from it by the outer ring road and its traffic.

We slowed as he drove into a street lined with speed bumps and I wound down the window to get some air. The cold blast made me shake my head. I noticed a patch of grass where a load of flowers had been left, to mark the place where another young person had been killed by a car.

'Nine years old, man,' said Tek Life. 'Me cyan't

unnerstan' why dem man must drive like pussyclaat aroun' side streets.'

'But you drive like a lunatic, man,' I said,
instantly regretting it.

Patrick shook his head. 'Pon de main road me
sometimes tek risk but me nevah drive fast around
side street — anywhere people deh me slow right
down, man.'

'OK,' I said.

'My baby brother get kill on de road by de
community centre,' he told me, making me feel
about ten centimetres tall.

'I'm sorry,' I said.

'Is cool, Billy. Me just makin' a point — him get
kill twenty year ago.'

'Still . . .'

He looked at me and nodded. 'But still . . .' he
agreed.

We got back in around two hours later: Tek Life's
pick-up took longer than expected. It was a three-
year-old girl called Liberty, Tek Life's youngest
child. We collected her at a flat on the estate and
then he drove around for a bit, grabbed some
money from one man, weed from the next and a
box full of cassette tapes from the third. I was
worried that all the ganja smoke in the car might
harm the little girl but she didn't even notice it. By

the time we dropped Liberty at her mum's flat on another estate, she had become my friend, laughing and giggling as I told her a stupid story about fairies and goblins, stoned to high heaven. As we joined Ellie and my mum in the kitchen, I asked Tek Life how many kids he had. He thought about it for a while before replying.

'Eight,' he said. 'Three bwoi and five gal – my princes and princesses, man.' He grinned so that his gold teeth showed.

'That's a lot of children,' said Ellie, as we sat down.

'The ones me know 'bout anyway,' he laughed. 'One a mi yout' dem live 'bout three streets away from here. On the other side of the main road.'

'Oh right – what's his name – I bet we know him,' I said.

Just then my mum interrupted and told us that we had curry to eat for dinner. Then she asked me to help her get things ready. Tek Life said he was going out again for a bit and asked if he could eat later. My mum smiled and shrugged.

'If you wanna heat it up later – be my guest,' she said.

'Seen,' grinned Tek Life. 'Me soon come.'

And then he slipped out again, off to do whatever it was that he did.

'Shit!' I said. 'Forgot my fags.'

'*Billy*—' began my mum.

'But I only went out with him to get some fags.'

'You should really give up, young man,' said Ellie.

'Yes,' agreed my mum.

'But you smoke,' I told her.

'Yeah – and I should stop too – it's a terrible habit.'

I grabbed my mum's pack from the table and opened the back door as she spoke.

'So you're not coming for one then?' I asked her with a smile.

'Oh well – if you're going to twist my arm,' she grinned.

'Stinky people,' moaned Ellie. 'You'll have bad breath and smelly hair and I won't kiss you.'

I raised an eyebrow. 'Were you planning on doing that?' I asked.

'*Was*,' replied Ellie, coming to the back door as I stood outside with my mum. 'And where's my present?'

I looked at my mum and winked. 'What present?' I asked.

'Oh, stop being funny – I hate it – you're just rubbish at it.'

'You'll get it tomorrow,' I told her. 'So be patient.'

'*Oh!*' she moaned, going back to the table.

'Can you stir my curry, Ellie?' said my mum.

'*Yeah*,' said Ellie excitedly.

'Without trying some, young lady,' warned my mum.

'As if I *would*,' said Ellie, as I spied her through the door, thinking she was out of sight and spooning some into her mouth.

TWENTY-SEVEN

Zeus was sitting in his basket looking almost his usual bored self when Della came through the back door with Sue. I was kneeling beside him, offering him a Mars bar that Ellie had given me, warm and squashed out of shape. He sniffed at it a few times before turning up his nose and going back to staring into space. I patted him on the head and gave the chocolate back to Ellie. Or at least I tried.

'Eurghhh – I don't want it back,' she told me. 'I shouldn't have given it to you.'

'You two are like kids,' said Della.

'One of us is,' I reminded her, nodding in Ellie's direction.

'Only until tomorrow,' she beamed. 'Then you have to treat me like an adult – remember?'

Della gave me a funny look.

'I promised to stop calling her kid and telling

her when to go to bed,' I told her.

'Yeah – right,' replied Della, smirking. 'You know, for someone who is quite clever, you ain't got no idea, have you?'

'About what?' I asked her.

'You'll soon work it out,' she told me, before giggling with Ellie.

We left my mum and Sue discussing what had gone on and headed into the living room. Ellie put the telly on and sat down, her feet tucked underneath her.

'I'm still hungry,' she said, not looking away from the TV.

'We only just ate, you greedy monkey.'

'I could eat summat too,' said Della.

'Never mind that,' I told her. 'How are you?'

She shrugged. 'I'm fine – why wouldn't I be?' she replied, without looking me in the eye.

'Della . . .'

'What?' she snapped. 'I'm fine. Things happen, Billy. It's cool.'

'He ain't got back to you yet then?' I asked.

'No – he ain't got back to me, but I wasn't expecting him to, Billy. In my head I've kind of dumped him anyway – I just wanted to tell him to his face.'

'Oh right,' I said.

'Now – if you've finished playing at being a

shoulder to cry on, I wanna watch the telly,' she told me.

I was about to ask some more questions but I knew her and knew her moods, so I left it alone. Instead I went outside and had another fag before chatting to Sue about things for a bit. When I got back to the living room, Della looked like she had been crying and Ellie had a red face.

'What's up?' I asked, like a dickhead.

'*Nothing!*' shouted Della. 'Jesus – how many times I got to tell you both?'

I looked at her and shook my head.

'Ain't us you wanna be shouting at,' I said. 'That ain't right.'

Della's eyes were blazing as I began to speak but turned watery as I finished. She knew that she was in the wrong but it took me telling her before she admitted it even to herself. She had always been that way. She got up and kissed Ellie on the cheek. 'I'm sorry,' she said.

Ellie looked up at her through tear-filled eyes and smiled. A bubble of snot broke out of her left nostril.

'Nah – my sister's got a snot-up nose,' teased Della.

'Shut up and get me a tissue, you witch,' said Ellie, half complaining and half smiling.

Della grabbed a tissue from the box on the table

and handed it to her. Then she came up to me and gave me a hug. 'Sorry,' she said.

'It's OK,' I told her. 'Things are kind of fucked up, aren't they?'

She nodded. 'It's like there's this thing with me and Jas and then all the crap that's happening with the rumours – makes you think that we're jinxed, don't it? Especially after what happened with that Busta.'

'Yeah,' I replied, wondering where it was all going to end.

I sat down and decided to change the subject, just to cheer everyone up. Especially Ellie.

'So what we doin' tomorrow?' I asked them both.

'At last – you've started talking about my birthday,' said Ellie. 'I wasn't gonna say anything but—'

'Shut up, Ellie, and tell us what you want to do,' I told her.

'Charming,' she replied, wiping a bit more snot away.

'We kind of decided to get pizza and DVDs and stay over here,' Della told me. 'Seeing as how you is hiding from the world,' she added.

I laughed. 'And when were you going to ask me?'

'It's only because you're a kind of invalid,' said Ellie, 'In a manner of speaking . . . You've still got to take me out properly when this is all over, and my present better be good because . . .'

I switched off for the rest of the sentence because I remembered I hadn't got her anything yet. When I focused on her again, she was looking at me like I was crazy.

'Are you on drugs?' she asked, looking awkward immediately after she'd said it because of what was going on with Jas.

'I had a few tokes on a spliff earlier,' I told her.

'Where's mine?' asked Della, smiling at Ellie to show her that she wasn't offended by her drug remark.

Ellie beamed back at her. 'So that's all sorted then. We've just got to tell William,' she said.

'I'll do that,' I told her. 'What time you want him to come over?'

'About eight-ish,' Della told me. 'And if Willy's coming we better get extra food and drink.'

'*Drink?*' I asked.

'*Yeah* – nuttin' heavy, Dad. Just a few beers. Relax, Billy.'

'Silly old man,' added Ellie.

I grabbed the cushion behind me and chucked it at her head.

My dad came by about nine o'clock with no news to report. He'd been out for most of the day, talking to people with Ronnie, and hadn't heard anything other than what Nanny had found out. Basically, everyone with an interest and loads of people without one were all pointing the finger at us. Most of them had seen the posters and had heard the whisper that was doing the rounds. My dad looked worried and I asked him if he was OK. He shook his head.

'This is gonna be tough, Billy. Nuff man talking . . .'

'Shit.'

'Yeah – most of the dealers are lying low and there's all kinds of rumours about who's gonna get lifted next.'

'It's worse than we thought, innit?' I said.

He nodded. 'And we ain't no closer to finding out who's behind it all. No one knows a thing about that – as far as they're concerned—'

'We're just making it all up and we're the informers, right?' I said.

'Yeah.' He nodded.

'So what now?' I asked.

'Same again tomorrow. Meantime keep my number on your recent call list – that way you can call me straight away if anything happens.'

I gulped down some air. 'You think it will?' I said.

'Yeah – it has to. These people wouldn't go to so

much trouble to let it lie now,' he said, repeating what Nanny had said.

The kitchen door opened and my mum came in. She looked at Lynden like he was a piece of shit.

'Lynden,' she said flatly. 'Not you again.'

'Rita – you all right?' asked my dad.

'Fine,' she said. 'I just came to grab a bottle of wine – don't let me interrupt you.'

'You're not,' he said.

'After all, sixteen years is a long time to make up for.'

Lynden sighed. 'Come nuh, sister – dem t'ings happen a long time ago—'

'Yeah – but they happened to us, didn't they? To me and Billy. You just went off and lived your life.'

'Rita—' he began, only my mum wasn't having it.

'Don't Rita me, you wanker!' she shouted. That was when I knew she was angry because she didn't like swearing.

'But—' he protested.

'But shit, Lynden. Just do what you need to do and get the fuck out of my house – run off back to whichever woman you're messing around now – just like you did all them years ago.'

And with that she turned and walked out, her head held high. I turned to my dad and shrugged.

'She's not happy with you,' I said, trying to

make a joke out of what had just happened.

'Yuh tellin' me,' he said. 'I'm gone, anyway – just remember to call if anything happens – you hear?'

'Yeah – I will,' I replied.

'Good,' he said, getting up and putting his hand on my shoulder.

'I'll see you tomorrow, OK?'

I nodded. As he left the house I wondered what tomorrow would bring. If I had known I would have made him stay.

TWENTY-EIGHT

Jas watched Dee as he chopped up lines of coke, desperate for some. His head was crawling with spiders and that sweet voice, the whisper that called to him all the time, sounded like it was a siren going off in his brain. He leaned over quickly and snorted two fat lines of white powder, hoping for the rush to be instant, like the first time. It wasn't. It took a while, but when it came it brought relief. He sat back in the passenger seat of the hired Golf and closed his eyes, sniffing hard. Dee laughed at him and did some himself.

Jas heard the engine start and felt the car pull away from the kerb. He didn't know where they were going next and he didn't care. He was happy now, ready to do whatever he needed to, wearing his favourite mask. When he opened his eyes he realized they were driving down a country lane, heading for Malk's house. The trees loomed in from both sides and the headlights created a tunnel of light through which they sped. He sat wide eyed and watched in silence. It was only when they arrived at Malk's house that he finally spoke, although he was sure that his words were slurred.

'What we doin' here?' he asked.

'Just gotta grab summat and give Malk the money in the boot,' replied Dee.

The money. In bundles – fifties and twenties – all of it inside three rucksacks. He smiled as he remembered the summer before, when he'd found something similar with Will. It seemed like it had happened in another life.

'Just wait here, bro, and grab a can of Red Bull off the back seat. You sound like you need it,' said Dee, leaving him in the dark driveway.

Jas looked up at the house, with its five front windows and three garages. One day he'd have one of these, he said to himself. He'd tell his mum to retire, take care of her and live life like the other man did. The man with the money. He turned on the stereo as he sat and thought and the familiar sound of *No Woman, No Cry* came out of the speakers. He sat back and closed his eyes again, remembering the way his mum had sung the same song to him when he was a toddler, changing the 'woman' to 'baby' so that he thought the song was about him. Different faces flickered in his mind.

His mum, when she was younger and didn't have the wrinkles she carried now. Billy on their first day at junior school, wearing a ganja T-shirt and Dr Martens with the Rasta flag on them, his hair shaved close to his scalp. Della looking up at him as they had sex, her mouth open slightly . . .

He opened his eyes again and turned off the music. Didn't like where it was taking him. Instead he opened the door, got out and stretched his legs. The night was chilly and he shivered as he stood by the car, but he didn't get back in.

'We gotta follow Malk back into town,' said Dee, reappearing and getting into the car. 'Just to watch his back – make sure there ain't no coppers around when he does the deal.'

Jas wondered what deal Dee was on about even as he nodded.

'Line up that pipe I gave you,' said Dee, starting the engine.

Jas pulled a foil wrap of rocks from his pocket and got the pipe ready.

Divy watched from a distance as two cars pulled up, a Black Golf GT TDi and a grey Peugeot 206. He was standing in the shadow of an old cricket pavilion, across a patch of grass from the gym car park where the deal was being done. He knew that Dee was in the Golf because he'd taken a ride in it earlier in the day. That meant that Malk was in the 206. He watched as the Golf circled the car park twice and then left. It went out of the gates and down a road by the university, coming to a stop on double yellows by some railings. That way Dee could see what was going on without being seen himself. Or so he thought. Divy grinned as he imagined the look on Dee's face when the police hit his brother. He moved back further into the shadows and waited.

Ten minutes after Malk had arrived, Divy was watching the ordinary gym members going in and out of the complex when he saw a silver Audi TT arrive. It pulled up behind Malk's car and idled. Divy moved forward just a touch, looking for the coppers. Where were they? A short balding man got out of the Audi and went and sat in the 206. Five minutes later he was still there and nothing had happened. The police were nowhere to be seen. Divy swore as he saw Busta's tight plan unravel at the seams. If the police didn't turn up he was in trouble. He told himself that he was being paranoid, that the coppers wouldn't let him down. Not when he'd told them how much cocaine was involved. He stood and tried to be patient.

Another five minutes passed before Malk got out of the 206 and went to the driver's side of the Audi. They were switching cars. Divy looked around at the gym members in the car park, ignoring the two cars and getting into their own, and he tried to work out if any of them were undercover. It was hard to know. Half of the blokes he'd seen going into and leaving the gym looked like they could be coppers. He started to panic. Then the Audi set off for the gate to the car park.

Divy was just about to start thinking up excuses for Busta when the police struck. A dozen 'gym members' converged on the 206, and from between some of the parked cars armed response officers stood and took aim, shouting instructions. Divy moved further forward and saw the Audi sandwiched between a police van and car, more armed response officers pointing guns at the window. He saw Malk get out and look around, ducking as he put his hands to his head. He looked over towards where Dee's Golf had been parked. It was gone. Divy turned and started to walk away, through the sixth-form college beyond the gym and down onto the main road. He was grinning like a madman.

Dee sped down the ring road, swearing over and over again. Jas felt his heart racing as they flashed past the other cars and flew through red lights. Only when they'd gone about two miles did Dee pull up outside an old boarded-up pub and get out. He was still swearing and began to punch the hired car over and over again. Jas got out and pulled him away as he started crying.

'I'm gonna kill them!' he shouted. 'I don't give a fuck who they are – I'm gonna find them and I'm gonna finish 'em!'

Jas struggled to hold his cousin and his own temper in check. They'd been set up. He breathed a sigh of relief that he hadn't been in the car. That Dee hadn't chosen to sit in on the deal. Even in his drug-addled state, Jas could see how bad it was. The Audi had five kilos of cocaine in its boot. That meant years in prison for his cousin, not to mention the thousands of pounds in the boot of the 206 – money that was lost for good. He let Dee go and went to sit down on the pavement.

'What are we gonna do?' he asked.

'Fucking kill them,' whispered Dee. 'Find out who they are and kill them.'

'What about Malk?'

Dee pulled out his phone. 'I'm gonna have to tell Kully,' he said. 'Shit . . .'

'You want me to do it?' asked Jas.

'What?'

'Ring Kully and sort out whoever did this,' replied Jas.

Dee sat down next to Jas and put his arm around Jas's shoulder. 'One thing at a time, bro, but thanks for offering. At least we know you ain't gonna let us down.'

Jas got out his mobile but Dee put a hand on it. 'Not yet,' he said. 'I need a hit first.'

TWENTY-NINE

Kully paced up and down the living room of the house he owned just down the road from Dee's place. Jas had expected him to rage at them but he had just nodded, said something about fixing up a lawyer for Malk and then wondered aloud how he was going to break the news to his dad. Jas ignored him and drifted in and out of consciousness, brought on by the brown he'd smoked to calm himself before he'd seen Kully. He was still pacing at just after five in the morning, when there was a knock at the door. Dee went to answer it and came back into the room with Divy.

'You got something to tell me?' demanded Kully.

'Yeah,' said Divy, nodding to Jas and Dee.

'*So?*'

'I know who's been doing all the grassing,' he replied.

208

'*Who?*' asked Dee, getting up off the leather sofa.

'You ain't gonna like it—'

'Just tell us, Divy,' snapped Kully, 'before I smash your head into the fucking wall.'

'It's Jas's old mates,' said Divy, watching Jas for a reaction.

Jas heard something but couldn't make it out. Instead he pretended to be OK and nodded. But he needed to close his eyes.

'Seems to me like he don't care anyhow,' Dee told Divy. 'He even offered to do 'em over earlier—'

'What – his *mates*?' asked Divy.

'Nah man – whoever informed on Malk – he's raring to get them,' corrected Dee. 'And even if they're his old pals like you say – he'll still do 'em.'

Divy watched the realization sink into Kully's brain and waited. Dee had warned him that Kully's temper wound up slowly like a spring. But when it went . . .

First Kully put his foot through the television screen. There was a pop followed by a bang, as shards of glass fell to the floor and smoke rose from the back of it. Then he grabbed a micro hi-fi and threw it at the wall, where it shattered and fell to the floor with a thud that cracked the laminate. Dee stood up to stop him and got a head butt for his trouble. Finally, Kully went into the long narrow kitchen and came back with a butcher's cleaver.

'Who?' he demanded. 'I want names . . .'

He swung the cleaver, ready to bring it down on Divy's head. Or so Divy thought.

'A dread bloke called Nanny and his stepkid – Billy. Apparently there's been posters all over the ghetto about him,'

Kully threw the cleaver to the floor, damaging more of the laminate. 'You sure?' he asked.

Divy nodded. 'Yeah – everyone knows it's them. They's so blatant that a female copper even visits them – a CID bitch called Elliot—'

Kully nodded. 'I know her,' he said. 'She had me in over some bullshit wounding charge – some boy that I glassed. She di'n't have no proof though.'

'Well, she's been seen going in and out their house – and now the dread has gone into hiding,' added Divy.

Kully seemed to calm instantly, as quickly as he had exploded. He walked over to his brother and pulled a handkerchief from his pocket, kneeling to wipe the blood from his nose.

'Sorry, bro,' he said to Dee, who just shrugged and then grinned.

'No prob – all of us is angry,' gasped Dee, as he tried to swallow the blood that was making its way down into his throat from his nasal cavity.

'Does it hurt?' asked Kully.

Dee nodded.

'Yo, Jas – fix my bro a hit will yer?' demanded Kully.

When Jas didn't reply, Kully turned to look at him. He was out cold. 'Best fix yer own,' he told Dee. 'An' do me one an' all.'

Then he turned to Divy. 'I'm gonna hit them,' he said, not blinking.

'How?' asked Divy.

'I'm gonna burn down their house with all of them inside,' he replied.

'I'll do it,' offered Dee.

Kully thought for a minute and then shook his head. 'Nah – but you can help,' he said. He turned to Divy. 'What about the dread?'

Divy grinned. 'If something happens to his family, he'll come out from wherever he is.'

'Ten grand, Divinder – you hit him – with a shooter,' offered Kully, whispering.

Divy smiled. The money would be a nice little nest egg. 'I'll do it,' he said without hesitation, 'and I'll go along with the other one too. For free.'

Just like the information I passed onto the police, he thought to himself.

Kully rummaged in his pockets for his coke. He pulled out a fat bag of it and handed it to Divy.

'Let's seal the deal,' he said, before turning to Jas, who was still asleep.

'Yow! Sleeping batty – *wake up*! We got work to do!' he shouted, kicking at him.

Jas stirred and looked around, unsure of where he was. His head was light and his stomach felt tiny. He sat up and blinked. 'What?' he asked.

'Just go and wash yer face or something,' ordered Kully. 'We got work to do.'

Jas went off to the bathroom as Divy and Kully sat down at a beech table from Ikea.

'You might have to drug his raas before he'll do anything,' Divy told Kully.

'Do what you have to,' replied Kully. 'I don't care as long as it gets done.'

Divy smiled. 'Seen . . .' he said, forming a plan.

THIRTY

By Tuesday lunch time I was bored out of my mind again. Tek Life had gone out, with my permission, saying that he was only going to see someone a few streets away. Things had been calm since the last attack and I wasn't overly worried. I said I'd call him if anything came up. My mum had given me a couple of crime novels to read, one by Michael Connelly and the other by James Lee Burke. I was halfway through the first one, which was set in Los Angeles and I was really enjoying it. It was about a serial killer called 'The Poet'. I'd drunk about six cups of coffee through the morning and smoked ten fags. I was hungry. I put down the book and made myself a sandwich, wondering if Lynden had found anything out. Then I decided to watch the lunchtime news.

I went into the living room and turned on the telly. There was yet another auction programme on, this one for houses, and I flicked channels until I'd finished my food and the BBC news came on. It was full of reports of death and war from around the world, followed by something from Parliament, where the two leaders of the main parties were arguing with each other over something really stupid. I turned over, disgusted by their antics. Politics was a joke. It was all about who could *say* the best things, not who *did* the best things, and all around me, every day, whether I was walking the neighbourhood or watching the news, I saw so much shit that needed sorting out, it made me angry. And all the politicians could do was get their hair done, their make-up just right, and try and score points from each other, in debates that most of the country didn't bother watching. It just made no sense.

I was about to go back to my book when the local news came on. That's normally when I switch right off, but I couldn't. The main headline was a story about a police raid on a major drug operation in our city. My heart sank when I heard the words and I sat down with a knowing feeling in my mind. It was something to do with us. The reporter talked about exclusive footage of a drug raid, released by the police to show that their hard-line drug policies were working. I watched as the grainy footage showed a gym, up by the university, and police swooping on a Peugeot 206, followed by an Audi TT. Then the shot cut back to the reporter.

'. . . *local businessmen David Higham and Malkit Singh are both being questioned by police and will appear in court this afternoon. Singh, a hosiery millionaire, recently appeared at a business lunch with the mayor. Police sources say that the haul was nearly five kilos of cocaine and tens of thousands of pounds. Police spokesperson Detective Inspector Charlie Morris publicly thanked the anonymous informant for his information and urged the rest of the public to follow suit. He called the latest raid an earthquake that would rock the local drug trade to its very foundations . . .'*

I didn't hear the rest. All I could think about were the words 'anonymous informant'. Exactly what we were being accused of. I sat back and let the potential consequences wash over me. So far, all the arrests that we'd been blamed for had been of street operators or middle men. This was someone near the top of the trade in the city. If the attacks escalated in line with the seniority of the dealer, we were in serious trouble. I ran into the kitchen and grabbed my phone, looking for my dad's number.

He answered on the second ring, like he already had his mobile in hand.

'I was just about to call you myself,' he said.

'You've seen it?' I asked.

'*Seen* it? Everyone in town knows about it and everyone is blaming Nanny.'

'But he's not even here,' I protested.

'That don't mean shit to anyone, kid. You at home?'

'Yeah,' I replied, feeling myself breaking into a cold sweat.

'Where's Tek Life? he demanded.

'Down the road – he should be back soon.'

'Call him and tell him to get back *now*,' he told me.

I could hear someone on another phone, some-where near my dad, shouting. 'Who's that in the background, Dad?' I asked.

'Ronnie – he's trying to calm down some of the people that work for us.'

'Shit . . .' I said.

'Exactly,' replied my dad.

'Who's this Malkit Singh anyway?' I asked.

'One of the brothers that you asked me about.'

'Oh . . .'

I wondered again whether he thought I really *was* the informant. After all, I'd only asked him to find out about Jas's cousins recently. But then I decided that I was being paranoid. What reason would either me or Nanny have to grass up anyone?

'Look, I've gotta go – call your mum and get your friends round to the house. Until I'm sure that nothing's gonna happen, I want you all where I can see you,' he added.

'You coming over then?'

'Later on – first I'm gonna send round a couple of lads. They'll be outside, in a car, watching the house.'

'Cool.'

'And Billy, no matter what happens – *don't* call no police, OK?'

'OK,' I replied.

I rang off and dialled Nanny's number but it went straight to answer and I remembered what he'd said about going to Brixton. In one respect, I was glad he was out of harm's way, but at the same time I could have done with him being at home too. I left a message for him to call me urgently and rang my mum at work, before going through the phonebook to call the rest of the Crew. We were all due to meet up for Ellie's birthday later anyway but I wanted to make sure that they knew something had happened. Just in case.

THIRTY-ONE

Tyrone sat in the freezing cold and watched the girls walking by the precinct. He had his hood up and his jacket zipped but the cold was still biting. He cussed Sean for making him wait outside for so long. Sean had called him earlier, left a message on his phone, asking to meet after school. Not that Sean had turned up for school. Now he hadn't even turned up for their meet and Tyrone was ready to go home to some warmth. He eyed the blonde girl who hung around with Billy's mates. The girl they had been paid to pick on. She looked like she was hurrying home. Tyrone wondered what was up with her and then watched as she crossed the road and headed for her own street. She was fit.

He stood up and was starting to leave the precinct when Sean came running up to him. He looked like he hadn't slept for a few nights and he stank of sour body odour. Tyrone stepped back from him as he spoke.

'Yes, Tee,' he said, grinning.

'I was just about to go – what do you want?' asked Tyrone.

'More work for that Divy,' said Sean excitedly. 'And check this – he's paying five hundred each for this one. *Five hundred!*'

Tyrone looked around and saw that a group of lads had heard Sean. '*Ssh!* Man – you want the whole place to know yer business?' he scolded.

'Forget them, man. We're meeting him at eleven to sort it out,' said Sean.

'Sort *what* out?' asked Tyrone.

'They done it again – them informer – and one of them Asian brothers has been pinched,' said Sean.

Tyrone looked around again. The lads were still listening. He grabbed Sean by the arm and pulled him away, in the direction of the library.

'Wha' yuh a do, man?' asked Sean, getting angry.

'You need to shut your battyhole mouth and come with me,' said Tyrone.

'Res' yuhself,' argued Sean.

'Listen – dem man over deh were listening to us – you don't want them to know yer business.'

Sean nodded and then started to tell Tyrone

what they were supposed to be doing. Tyrone listened, knowing that Divy was the informant, and at the end shook his head.

'I ain't doin' it,' he told Sean.

'Wha' yuh mean? It's five hundred notes, bro,' replied Sean. 'Yuh mad?'

Tyrone shook his head. 'I ain't mad and I definitely ain't your bro, so tek yuh money and gwan,' he said.

'Nah – don't be like that, Tee. We ain't doing shit to make the dough—'

Tee grabbed Sean around the throat and shoved him into the fencing around the library. He looked over to the precinct, to make sure that the lads saw him attacking Sean.

'I ain't doin' that,' he spat. 'Yuh call that nuttin'? I ain't goin' jail for no informer.'

'But—' said Sean, as Tyrone let him go.

'But nuttin' – now leave me alone,' replied Tyrone.

'Yuh gonna be the next one then,' threatened Sean.

Tyrone looked at Sean, shook his head and then headbutted him. Sean sank to his knees, holding his nose. Tyrone knew that he was being watched with more interest now and he punched Sean in the side of his head, knocking him to the left.

'I ain't yuh bro and I ain't no member of your

crew. Is your bwoi, Divy, the informer – yuh get me?'

Only Sean didn't get him: he was out cold. Tyrone turned and walked past the group of lads, who looked at him in awe. One or two of them whispered stuff as he passed by. He turned to them and scowled.

'Dat bwoi Divy is the real informer,' he said to them. 'Mek sure yuh a pass it on.'

Then he turned and headed home, ready to call his dad and put an end to the whisper that he had started with the help of the knob lying sparked out on the concrete behind him.

THIRTY-TWO

Tek Life flipped his mobile shut and shook his head.

'It wasn't Nanny,' he told me. 'Just my son.'

'Oh, right,' I replied.

'I man haffe go check him right now – him want to tell me somet'ing.'

I nodded. 'Yeah – that's cool – you can't be here twenty-four hours a day,' I told him.

Tek Life said that he'd be back as soon as he could and left to go and speak to his son.

I went into the kitchen and made myself yet another cup of coffee. I couldn't concentrate on anything for longer than a few minutes. My head was taken up with the latest drug arrests and what my dad had told me about them being linked to us. My mum was also due home soon and I was hoping she had remembered to get Ellie's present for me. And that she'd turn up before Ellie did. I picked up *The Poet* and read some more, trying hard to get lost in the plot so that I'd stop worrying about things, but it didn't work.

Instead I ended up thinking about Jas. Did he think that we were the ones who'd grassed up his cousin? Was he part of the conspiracy to frame us with it? I realized that the second part was nonsense. No matter how estranged Jas had become from the rest of us – and it was becoming one of those situations that couldn't be turned back – he would never do anything to hurt us. It just wasn't in him. I saw the way he was with us all. Remembered everything we had been through. It wasn't something you could just throw away.

I sat and thought about the first time I'd seen him, back when we started junior school. I had a skinhead and thought I was really cool in an over-sized ganja T-shirt that I'd nicked from my mum and Dr Martens boots. My jeans had been really battered, with paint splattered on them. Jas had been tall even then, and skinny with it. He had tram lines razor-cut into his hair and was into hip-hop, big time. We were put in the same class and ended up sitting together, and that had been it. From day one we became the best of friends and when I introduced him to Will we became a gang.

We did everything together. Playing football,

fighting, fancying the same girls, the lot. It was like we had been made to complement each other, even down to when we argued, with one of us always acting the peacemaker. And we never did that two-against-one thing like so many of the other threesomes in school, where one person was shunned for some stupid reason for a month at a time. By the time we hit secondary school, Della and eventually Ellie had joined in too and we were the way we are now. Or, more accurately, the way we *were*. I missed Jas. Missed his stupid jokes and his temper and his baggy, no-ass jeans that I took the piss out of. Missed his friendship, which felt like it was gone for good. And that hurt.

When my mum got in, just after half-five, she was carrying a little bag from a gift shop in town. Ellie's present.

'You get it then?' I asked.

'Yeah – it's really lovely. Did you choose it yourself?' she asked, looking impressed.

'Yeah – Ellie likes stuff like that.'

'She likes you too, Billy,' grinned my mum.

'Not how you think,' I replied, not wanting to get into it. I wanted to talk about the other stuff.

'I don't think anything – I *know*. It's obvious and she is very beautiful.'

I shrugged. 'She's also about to be only fifteen.'

'So?' asked my mum. 'How many girls her age you know of with older boyfriends?'

'Er . . . loads but—'

'So there you go. You're only just over a year older than her. You only just made it into your school year, you know. You could have been there still,' she teased.

'And your point, old woman, is what?'

My mum shrugged. 'If you like her you shouldn't worry about her age. You can wait for all the messy stuff until her *next* birthday—'

'*Mum!* That's not even what I was thinking—'

'Oh suit yourself, kid. I was just trying to talk to you.'

I put down my book, which I hadn't noticed I was still holding, and looked at Ellie's present. It was cool. Then I turned back to my mum.

'Never mind trying to fix me up with Ellie – did you get my message?'

'Yes,' she said, opening a cupboards and pulling out her stash of curry spices.

'What you doin'?' I asked.

'Making chicken curry – why?'

'I thought we was all having pizza and stuff?'

'We are. Marge is making the pizzas, Sue's bringing a load of cakes and stuff, and I'm making curry and rice – Ellie asked me to.'

'Right . . .'

'And Will is going to bring a load of fried chicken wings with him – it's a real family effort.'

I got up, opened the back door and lit a fag. 'Someone else got nicked today,' I told my mum.

'Yes – I know that,' she replied, like she didn't understand how serious it was.

'And we're getting the blame,' I added.

'You told me that too,' she continued nonchalantly.

'So – aren't you even a *bit* worried about it?' I snapped.

She looked up at me with her big brown eyes, sighed and then put the spices down. Then she walked over and stood right in front of me.

'I *am* worried, Billy, but what do you want me to do – stop living my life?'

'Just be a bit more concerned, that's all,' I told her.

'I *am*. But I'm not letting some stupid rumour ruin my life, kid. I've *been* on those streets and I've seen plenty of shit but I'm not *scared* of anybody – you understand? If they want to come and have a go at us, that's fine – I can't stop them. But I'm *not* gonna just lie down and die if they do.'

She had a fire in her eyes when she'd finished speaking and for about the fifth time in the last twelve months I felt so proud of my mum and her courage that I nearly cried.

'And don't be doing no cryin' either,' she teased.

'Shut up,' I replied, pretending that she was wrong.

'*And* we've got Tek Life around as well as your dad – and regardless of what I think of Lynden, he's a bloody good person to call on when you need help.'

I nodded. 'I'm beginning to get that impression,' I said.

'When I was with him he was respected and that was *before* he joined the real criminals.'

'Is that what he is then?' I asked, although it was a stupid question. I could gloss over it all I liked but my dad was involved in breaking the law. It was what he did. But he was still my dad.

'You *know* what he is,' she told me. 'Get to know him, by all means, but be ready for some heart-break along the way, Billy. It's the nature of the business he's in – I *know*.'

I nodded.

'And be ready for surprises too – that man is full of them.'

She left it at that, took two drags from my cigarette and returned to her cooking. I sat at the table and watched her, like I used to when I was a little kid, and I smiled to myself.

★ ★ ★

227

Ellie turned up with her family at about half past six. She was beaming from ear to ear and giggling with her brother. Her parents stayed in the kitchen, where my mum opened a bottle of wine, and we made our way into the living room, where Chris turned on the telly straight away.

'It's *The Simpsons*,' he explained.

'Yeah – that's wicked,' I agreed, sitting down to watch.

Ellie looked at me expectantly. 'Where is it, then?' she asked.

'Where's what?' I replied, not looking at her.

'Oh stop being a wanker and get my present,' she demanded.

'No need to swear,' I said.

'I'll swear if I want to – you do it all the time,' she reminded me.

'OK, OK,' I said to her, before looking at Christopher. 'Man, she's like a spoilt brat,' I told him.

Chris looked at me, shrugged and said that she normally opened his Christmas and birthday presents before he got a chance. I shook my head, turning back to his sister.

'You're so out of order. You can't open your brother's presents.'

She grinned. 'Don't change the subject, old man.'

I went into the kitchen to get her present, stopping on purpose to chat with her parents for a bit. When I got back into the living room she was almost ready to explode with impatience. Before I had the chance to give her the bag, it was out of my hands and being torn apart. Like a piranha tears apart flesh.

Then she saw what it was and her face went all red. She rushed over to me and gave me a hug, not letting go until I was almost out of breath.

'You got the one I told Della about! It's the same one!' she said.

I nodded. Her present was a silver ring with a purple stone set into it. It had cost me thirty quid, and I was about to get sacked at work for not going in, but it was cool and the look on her face was worth every penny. She was over the moon. She put it on and held her hand out in front of her, showed it to Christopher and then jumped on me, kissing me about six times before telling me that she loved me and running out of the living room to show her parents. I turned to Christopher.

'She's nuts, you know,' I said to him.

He nodded and then grinned. 'Your problem,' he told me. 'Or at least it will be.'

And then he turned back to the screen and told

me to be quiet because he was trying to watch his programme.

'You cheeky monkey,' I said to him, realizing that it obviously ran in the family.

THIRTY-THREE

Divy took the small handgun that Kully had given him and hid it in the boot of the Nova SR he had bought for two hundred notes from a mate. He looked at his fake licence, which had cost forty quid, and smiled. Then he jumped into the car, started it up and sped off to go and pick up Sean. He also wanted to catch up with Tyrone, hoping that he'd be hanging around the streets, to teach him a lesson. He rang Dee as he drove, speeding through the cold, dark night.

'You ready?' he asked.

'Whenever,' answered Dee on the other end of the line.

'I'll bring Sean round about midnight,' said Divy.

'Best make it eleven,' Dee told him, ringing off.

Dee threw the phone into Jas's lap and asked him if he was OK. Jas nodded but didn't speak. He couldn't. The mixture of heroin and cocaine he had just snorted made his muscles clench and relax without his control. He nodded again, but his brain was going haywire. The whisper had really caught him this time, made him worse than he had ever been, and he didn't like the feeling. He knew that it was the only way to stem the anger that he was feeling over his cousin getting nicked – taking more and more drugs – but it still felt wrong. He felt like he was becoming a stranger even to himself.

'Just ride it out, bro,' Dee told him. 'Tonight, we're gonna get even.'

Dee slipped a CD into the player and set off to pick up what they would need. He hoped that the lads he'd called had everything ready because he was in no mood to be messed about. The sounds of a hip-hop mix made the speakers pound as Dee drove over to the other side of the city. The city centre passed in a blur. They took the ring road left, past a predominantly Asian shopping quarter and on into the north end of the city. At a main set of lights he took a right and turned immediately left into an estate of low-rise blocks. He pulled up outside the largest and got out, leaving Jas where he was and dodging past the burned-out remains of a car, through the door to the building. He jogged up two flights of piss-stinking stairs and knocked on a steel door. When it opened he smiled.

'You done 'em?' he asked.

'Doin' 'em now,' said a short, squat Asian lad. 'Come in.'

Divy pulled up across the road from the precinct and got out of the Nova. He checked up and down the street and saw some of his dealers, standing by a lowered Honda Civic, old shape. He walked over.

'Easy,' he said to them.

'All right, Divy,' said the first lad, Martin. 'Summat wrong?'

Divy shook his head. 'Not yet,' he said. 'I'm looking for Tyrone, hangs out with Sean. You know him?'

The second lad, Ashiq, nodded. 'We was told he mashed up Sean good.'

'Yeah, Sean told me,' said Divy. 'Where's this Tyrone at?'

Both of them shrugged.

'Dunno – might be he's gone home, innit,' suggested Ashiq.

'If you see him, hold him and call me. There's money in it.'

'No problem,' replied Martin.

'Although, you know whose kid he is, don't you?' asked Ashiq.

Divy shrugged and told Ashiq that he couldn't care less. Ashiq told him anyway.

Divy left them where they were and went to pick up Sean, the new piece of information swimming around in his brain. He didn't know whether it was funny, serious, or a bit of both, but it would make things interesting . . .

Jas opened the boot of the old Citroën Xantia, and watched Dee place the box of bottles carefully inside. The bottles were capped and secured with fabric that was stuffed down the sides, to hold them in place and act as fuses. Jas looked at his cousin.

'What's that?' he asked.

'What we need, bro, to deal with them informers once and for all.'

'Right – so we know who they are,' he said, getting more confused than he already was.

'We found out last night but you was out cold, bro,' Dee told him.

'So who are they?' asked Jas, as a rush caught him and went straight to his head. He shivered.

'Never mind – it's better if we don't tell you, in case any of us get caught,' said Dee. 'You can't tell the coppers what you don't know, right?'

Jas shrugged. 'Why would I tell the police anything?'

'Just in case,' reassured Dee. 'It's to protect you, bro. We don't want another member of the family getting sent down.'

Jas nodded and closed the boot before getting back into the Xantia. Dee joined him and pulled a wrap from his pocket.

'Forget about your worries, bro. Let's do a few and then we'll get on with it.'

Jas eyed the wrap and smiled. 'It don't matter who they are,' he told Dee. 'Them bastards deserve all they get.'

Dee winked at him. 'You know it, bro. Better than you think, too.'

Jas watched him rack out lines on a CD cover and closed his eyes.

THIRTY-FOUR

Lynden came by at just after nine, telling me that he hadn't found out anything new. He told me that he was going to talk to some more people and would call me later. Then he had an argument with my mum and left. Will turned up with Della and Sue while they were arguing and we went into the living room, where Ellie had her feet up and was watching the telly. Her family ate early and had left just before my dad arrived. We waited until things had calmed down in the kitchen before piling in and starting on a load of food. My mum and Sue went out into the garden to have a smoke and chat about things, as they put it, as Will demolished a plate of curry and rice like he was eating a bag of crisps. Then he started on a pile of chicken wings and coleslaw. He saw me and Ellie watching him and grinned.

'What?' he shrugged. 'I'm a big lad and I need

my calories. Just because you two eat the same as a sparrow—'

'Yes,' said Ellie, 'but we do it in style. You might as well be shovelling that stuff down your throat.'

'I'll bloody shovel summat down your—' he began, but Ellie was in fighting mood.

'Uh-uh, Willy. You can't threaten me on my birthday – I'll cry,' she said, putting on a pathetic, girlie voice.

'Bwoi – leave some ah dat shit for us too,' warned Della.

'I've only had a bit,' Will said, looking at the pile of bones on his plate.

I looked at him and laughed. He was known for the messy way he ate and we wouldn't have had him any other way, I don't reckon.

'So what we gonna do when Mr Big Gut has finished?' asked Della.

'Watch lots and lots of DVDs,' announced Ellie. 'And drink lots and lots of alcohol.'

'Did you bring some,' I asked Della, who grinned at me.

'Course – Sue let me have some of her stash,' she said.

She got up and opened the fridge door to show me a whole load of booze. There was white wine, lager and a whole range of mixer drinks like Smirnoff Ice and Bacardi Breezers. I grinned.

'Well, what you waiting for? Chuck us a Bud.'

'Anyone else?' asked Della.

'Smirnoff Ice,' said Ellie. 'Pleaaase.'

'Mmmmmmmmmnnn,' mumbled Will through a mouthful of pizza.

'What?' asked Della.

Will swallowed his food and tried again. 'I don't like booze, but seein' as it's yer birt'day I'll have a lager,' he told her, grabbing another chicken wing.

'*What?* You said *all* of that with your mouth stuffed full of pepperoni pizza,' said Ellie.

'Mmmnnnnnnn,' mumbled Will, before spitting out a bone.

'You're disgusting,' Della told him as she gave him his beer.

'No I ain't — I just eat like a man,' he replied.

'Yeah — like Neanderthal man,' teased Ellie.

'Listen — just 'cos it's your birt'day don't mean I won't gi' you a slap,' joked Will.

'Like to see you try,' smirked Ellie. 'I bet you won't move for a day — you'll end up on one of those US talk shows: they'll need a crane to get you into the studio though, and you won't be able to catch a plane because you'll be sooo fat — you'll have to take a boat . . .' she continued.

'A big raasclaat boat, too,' added Della.

'I never knew it was "Pick on the William" day,' I said, trying to protect my oldest friend from a two-pronged assault.

'We can always start on you,' said Ellie. 'With your skinny legs and big ears—'

I held up my hand in submission. 'OK, OK. I just saw the calendar. It *is* "Pick on Willy" day,' I said.

'Don't be talking 'bout no willies at the table, Billy – I'm trying to eat,' protested Della.

'Oh for fuck's sake,' I groaned, getting up to go and have a fag.

When I walked back in they were still at each other and I suggested that we move into the living room to watch at least one of the five DVDs that Ellie had borrowed. Like we'd get a chance to watch all five anyway. Strange bird. We picked a movie all of us had seen before but one that we all liked. Ellie put it in and we turned off the lights as it started. Me and Ellie sat together on one sofa and Will and Della sat on the other. About half an hour into it, Will and Della went and got more drinks. Then we all sat and spoiled the film, competing to tell each other when the next funny bit was coming up. In the end we turned it off and Ellie asked if she could have another drink. Della winked at her and said that no one was counting. Ellie smiled. By eleven I was a bit drunk and Ellie and Della were giggling continuously. Will nodded at the door.

'Got one of them cancer sticks for me?' he asked.

'I didn't know you smoked,' I said, joking.

Will was one of those annoying people who only smoked when he was a bit drunk, and always asked for your last but one fag. Luckily for me, I had my mum's stash to raid and I went out the back with him, where we stood in the cold and talked nonsense for a bit, as the smoke from the cigarettes joined the fog of our breath.

When we got back inside, Della and Ellie were raiding the fridge for cold pizza and curry. Ellie loved eating cold curry, something I had never understood, and I laughed as she shoved spoonfuls of it into her mouth, getting it all over her chin. We went back into the living room and settled down again, this time to watch some American comedy thing set in a high school. It was rubbish but we still had fun. So much so that I totally forgot about my dad saying that he would call – and about Nanny promising to call Ellie to wish her a happy birthday.

And then, as we were messing about with cushions, Ellie leaned over and kissed me full on the lips. I nearly pulled back but I didn't. Before I knew it we were kissing again. When I looked up, Will and Della had left the room and I realized that I had been set up. The strange thing was – and

I didn't think it would happen that way – I didn't mind. I really didn't. Our relationship was just like that of any boyfriend and girlfriend anyway – without the 'messy stuff', as my mum had put it. I was just worried what people would think about her only being fifteen.

Ellie looked at me and smiled. 'I've wanted to do that ever since I met you,' she told me.

'I kind of knew,' I told her. 'I just thought you had a crush that would go away.'

'I knew you'd say that. It really does bother you that I'm a *whole year* younger than you, doesn't it?' she said. 'It's nothing.'

I nodded. 'Yeah – I know it's silly, but if I'm honest it does bother me. I *do* like you though. I think you're beautiful,' I told her.

She beamed at me. 'My mum thinks it's OK,' she told me. 'So it can't be that bad – she likes you.'

'You told your *mother*?' I asked.

'*Yeah* – we planned this together, along with your mum and Della. Oh, and Sue and my dad and Christopher—'

'*Ellie!*'

'Oh, quit complaining, you *girl*,' she said, kissing me on the cheek this time. '*You* wouldn't have made a move if I hadn't.'

She stood up and brushed down her clothes.

'Come on – let's go see what those two are doing,' she ordered.

I shook my head, stood up, wondered again whether I was doing the right thing, and then followed her out of the room.

THIRTY-FIVE

Jas sat back in the passenger seat and tried to forget about the burning sensation in his sinuses. His eyes were aching and the blood in his head seemed to be pounding its way round his brain, hammering at his skull. He closed his eyes and tried to think clearly. Lights danced on the back of his eyelids, purples and oranges and reds. He opened his eyes and the whisper began again. It had started as a soothing, calming voice with an edge of promise. Like the dulcet tones of a beautiful woman with perfect skin and cherry-scented breath. But slowly it had changed to a constant drone. Now, when he needed to silence it, the whisper was amplified in his mind, and only more of the same thing made it go away. He looked across at Dee.

'I need some more,' he told him.

Dee grinned and pointed to the glove

compartment, where he had left a wrap of heroin and cocaine in deadly combination.

'Help yourself, Cos – but just for tonight. From tomorrow, I think you need to take a break. That thing is taking you over, bro. You need to get it sorted.'

Jas opened the compartment in a hurry and took out the wrap. He took a CD case and held it flat. Opening the wrap, he piled the powder up and cut it into fat lines with a blade. He took the silver pipe from its hiding place in his jacket and bent forwards to make the whisper go away. Once, twice. Again and again, until his nose burned and his eyes watered. He retched but held it down and sat back in the seat.

From behind him Sean let out a laugh. 'You want some a dis spliff?' he asked him.

Jas turned and took the spliff. He drew hard three times and let the smoke into his lungs. Then he did it again. And again. He exhaled finally and passed the thing back. Time seemed to slow right down and he closed his eyes to the world . . .

In the back of the Xantia, Sean grinned to himself. The bwoi was off his tree, properly. He didn't even know what day it was. Sean realized that Divy's instructions would be easy to carry out. Let Jas do the first bit and then make sure that he did

the second bit himself. The state Jas was in it would
be a piece of cake. He took a pull on his spliff and
thought about the money and what he was going
to spend it on. He needed new trainers for a start,
and a new jacket, maybe a couple of hooded tops.
Then he'd take his girl out properly, get his hair
cut. Maybe even get himself a new girl . . . He
watched Dee driving silently around town,
doubling back on himself, taking the ring road
again and again, killing time.

'When we getting there?' Sean asked him.

Dee looked at him in the rear-view mirror. 'Ten
minutes,' he said. 'Maybe fifteen. We'll do it around
quarter to one.'

'Is my man goin' to be OK?' asked Sean.

Dee looked at Jas and then nodded. 'He'll be
fine,' he said. 'I'll give him a boost in a minute –
he's just tired, that's all.'

'Long as he's got my back,' replied Sean.

'Yeah, and you better have his,' warned Dee, 'or
you got me to deal with, unnerstan'?'

'Yeah,' smirked Sean.

Like it mattered anyhow, he thought to himself.

Jas heard them talking but couldn't make out what
they were saying. He felt disconnected from the
rest of the world, like he was floating on his own.
He looked down at his hands, held them in front

of his face. Then he looked out of the window at the streets flying by and thought about Della and the first time they had kissed. He smiled to himself for a moment before the burning in his nose took over again and he winced. He tried to clear his sinuses by sniffing hard and a wedge of congealed powder caught the back of his throat, making him retch again. Again he kept down the little that was in his stomach and let yet another rush take over his body. He didn't know where he was or what he was doing, but at that precise moment he didn't give a fuck either . . .

THIRTY-SIX

Tyrone looked on as his dad changed into a different shirt before heading out again. He stood and watched and tried to work up the courage to tell him what he knew. He waited until his dad was dressed before speaking.

'I seen you outside some house on Sunday afternoon,' he said.

His dad shrugged. '*And?*'

'A lad called Billy lives there,' he added.

His dad raised an eyebrow. 'You know Billy?' he asked.

Tyrone looked away and worked up some more courage. 'Yeah – I know him,' he said. 'How do *you* know him?'

'He's— Never mind that – he's in some trouble. Why are you asking?'

Tyrone gulped down air. 'Is it about the informers?' he asked.

'*Yeah* — you *know* something, kid?' asked his dad.

'Er . . . kind of,' he said. 'They've been getting shit off some people.'

Tyrone saw his dad let out a breath. 'People that *I'm* looking for,' he told his youngest son.

'These people — they've been paying kids to spread rumours about that lad — Billy — and his stepdad.'

'Nanny?'

Tyrone nodded.

'You know who they are, *don't* you?' said his dad.

Tyrone didn't answer.

'Talk to me, kid. Me nah go get mad but I have to know.'

'Why?' asked Tyrone.

'It's business,' his dad replied, hoping to hide the truth.

'*Why?*' repeated Tyrone.

'Yuh nuh mek *demand* of *me*, bwoi,' he snapped. 'Yuh know somet'ing, yuh better seh so — *now*!'

Tyrone stood his ground. 'Why's it so important to you anyway? It ain't like they're part of our family, is it?' he shouted back.

'*What* do you know?' his dad asked in a calmer voice.

'I was one of the people who did all that shit,' admitted Tyrone, looking down at his feet.

'You what? *You . . . ?*'

'I'm sorry — I didn't know. I thought they was really the informers,' he replied, trying to defend himself.

'Who got you to do it?' asked his dad, realizing that he was going to get more out of his son if he calmed down again.

'Some lad called Divy — it was just stupid stuff to begin with — just shouting and knockin' over bins and that—'

'You the one who cut up the dog—?'

'*No!*' protested Tyrone. 'I wouldn't do that.'

His old man shook his head. 'I don't fucking believe this,' he told Tyrone. 'What *else*?'

Tyrone sat down. 'The lad, Divy, he's the real grass. I heard him on the phone to some man called Busta — said everything was going to plan. I think he set up everything and now they're going after that Billy and his family—'

'Who?'

'Divy — he's been working for them Asian brothers — you know, the one that got nicked yesterday?'

Again his dad shook his head in disbelief. 'What are they going to do?' he asked Tyrone.

'Firebomb their house,' whispered Tyrone. 'And Divy's got a gun to shoot Nanny with — they asked me to go along but I said no.'

Lynden felt his temper rising. He grabbed Tyrone around the collar and pulled him to his feet so that they were face to face.

'*So why didn't you go with them?*' he spat at his son. 'And why tell *me*?'

Tyrone replied through tears. 'Because I never thought it would go this far and I was ashamed – I didn't want to hurt no one – not like that. I'm sorry, Dad. I'm ashamed . . .'

Lynden let his son go. 'You *should* be,' he told him. 'You helped to fuck up your own *brother*.'

Tyrone's mouth fell open and he sat in shock for a minute or two, as his dad made a phone call. No one replied. He looked at his dad through tear-filled eyes. He couldn't believe what he had heard. Couldn't believe that he hadn't known. Hadn't been told. That he'd caused his own brother so much grief. He began to get angry.

'Why didn't you tell me?' he demanded.

'Never mind that now,' replied Lynden, dismissing him. 'Get your jacket – we gotta get round there. You better *pray* them man ain't done nuttin' yet.'

THIRTY-SEVEN

Jas moved forward like an old man, having to think about putting his left foot in front of his right, and right in front of left. He held onto the bottles, one in each hand, and tried to see what was in front of him. His mind was a mess of emotions and rushes and there was that whisper again, teasing him, egging him on. The heat from the flames seared his face and forearms as he walked and he couldn't think straight. Something in his head told him that he was walking down a path he had been on many times in his life. There was something familiar about everything around him but at the same time it was new. Like looking at your favourite picture through someone else's eyes. He looked down at the burning petrol bombs that he held and raised them.

The window was two metres away, then one. He could hear his own breathing and shouts from behind. Someone was shouting, 'Throw them! Throw them!' The whisper became a laugh that repeated itself over and over and over again, mocking him, until he wanted to tear it out of his head . . .

Sean watched Jas stagger to the window. He was taking too long. They were gonna get caught. He lit the cloth fuse on the bottle he was holding and held it ready. The flame flickered and burned in the wind. He looked at Jas again. He was just standing where he was, like an idiot. What was he waiting for? Sean looked around to see if Dee was watching but he had parked the car a hundred metres down the street.

'Throw them, you knob! *Throw them!*' Sean shouted.

Jas turned to look at him and Sean could have sworn he was crying. He shouted again – the bottles were about to explode in Jas's hands. Jas turned and raised the bottles. Sean raised his own and threw it. He was going to run. That was what his head was telling his legs. But his legs didn't move. Instead he just stood and watched as the flames grew stronger and Jas began to scream . . .

The flames flicked higher and higher up Jas's jeans until he felt them melting to his legs. He screamed but to his mind no sound came from his mouth. He lurched forward, dropped the two bottles he was carrying and fell into their flames too, smashing the front window of the house with his forehead and slumping to the ground. The heat was getting stronger and stronger and the whisper that he had carried with him for the last few months, his constant companion, his reason for living, faded away as he dropped into unconsciousness . . .

THIRTY-EIGHT

I was kissing Ellie again when I heard the shouts. I thought they were coming from a load of youths or drunks.

'What's that?' she asked me.

'Dunno,' I replied. 'Forget about it — it's probably just kids pissin' about.'

I ignored them and carried on but they got louder and then I heard screams followed by breaking glass. I let Ellie go, pulled on my T-shirt and ran downstairs.

I heard more screaming, this time from women, and I jumped down the last ten steps, landed with a jolt and saw flames. I ran towards them, trying to think even as my brain went haywire. I needed something to put them out. I turned and ran back the way I had come, past a startled Zeus and out into the yard. I jumped the dwarf wall that separated my garden from Ellie's and slammed my bare foot against her dad's shed door. It flew open. I reached inside and grabbed the fire extinguisher that he kept for emergencies, turned and ran back through the house.

I could hear Della screaming and sobbing outside but I ran into the front room and let the extinguisher loose on the flames that were licking the window. I hit them at their base and watched as they fought at first and then died. The window was completely shattered and the frame was ruined. I began to get angry. I couldn't believe what was happening. I heard more shouts and screams. Heard Tek Life telling Della to get back. Get back. Wondering what was going on, I went outside, as the street filled with people and sirens wailed somewhere close by.

I saw the ashen faces of my mum and my best mate. I saw Della being held back by Ellie's dad and Tek Life, her face streaming with tears and wide eyed in shock. Ellie, in her T-shirt and pyjama shorts, hiding her face in her mum's chest. I saw tears, smelled petrol fumes and the charred scent of a barbecue gone wrong. It was like I was in a dream . . .

I saw my dad pull up in his car and jump out with that lad Tyrone, the one who didn't like me. I wondered what they were doing here together. And then, even though I tried to put it off, I turned to see what everyone was looking at, pointing at. Crying over . . .

There was a blanket covering part of someone's body and it was smoking. It was a charred, smoking, blistered, red and black mess. Where there should have been feet there were stumps, badly burned. I looked at Della and then back at the person on the floor outside my house. I don't know exactly how but I knew who it was straight away.

I moved forward and knelt down. I heard my mum shout 'No!' at me but I ignored her. I pulled away the blanket to look at Jas's face, to make sure that it was him. It was . . .

The skin had peeled back and cracked, exposing blackened tissue and gums. His hair was gone completely and one of his eyes was a bloody, burned mess. I tried not to look too closely but I couldn't help it. I sat back and put my head in my hands.

He started to shake. At first it was gentle but then it got stronger and stronger and I heard him moan. I stood up and grabbed my dad.

'He's alive – he's alive – get a fucking ambulance!'

My dad held me to him and wouldn't let me go. 'It's coming up the street now,' he told me.

I raised my head and looked past him. Towards the ambulance and the coppers and the fire engine. I looked at Tyrone, who stood with his head down, and even in all my grief and my shock, I wondered what he was doing with my dad. What he had done to make things the way they were. Then I pushed my dad away and went to my mum, who was standing with a shocked expression on her face. I stood with her for a moment, felt for her hand. And then I started to cry.

LATER

The two days after Jas died were a waking night-mare. I spent them staggering around in a daze, not understanding what had happened or why it had happened. And it wasn't just me. Will and Ellie wore the same haunted look that I had, and Della stayed away from everyone except Sue and the police, when they came to question her. She didn't answer her phone or reply to messages. She wanted to be left alone.

The police turned up behind the ambulance and immediately cordoned off the entire street. Lucy Elliot was with them, and once she had left Sean with another detective, she spent a long time with my mum, talking to her and comforting her. Then she asked if anyone knew what had happened. I was standing in the same spot I'd been in for ages, unable to speak. And then my dad, standing with Tyrone, asked me if I was OK. I didn't reply.

Elliot gave my dad and Tyrone a funny look and asked them who they were. My dad looked at my mum and then at me. He mouthed the word 'sorry' and then told her.

'I'm his dad,' he said, looking towards Tyrone before nodding in my direction. 'And I'm his dad, too.'

Elliot looked at me and then at my mum. My mum shook her head and walked away, towards Ellie and Will. I stayed where I was, watching Tyrone and wondering why I hadn't seen it earlier. There had been something about him when we'd first clashed, way back when I was looking for the people who had mugged me. Something in his eyes and in the way he spoke and held himself. He was almost the spitting image of my dad.

I also knew then that he was one of the lads who had mugged me. I realized that the reason I hadn't remembered their faces was that the only one I had looked at properly was Tyrone's. Maybe my subconscious hadn't wanted me to know that he was my brother. Maybe some kind of shock had made me forget. But now it was as clear as day.

Everything else moved quickly. Elliot called in Divy's description and then asked where Nanny was. My mum said that she hadn't spoken to him but would. When she called he was already on his way back and said that he would come straight home. I looked for Tek Life but he was nowhere to be seen. It was later that I found out he had gone after Divy himself. In fact it was Tek Life who found him, despite the police having more people on the case. Tek Life had just called around, found out where he lived and gone. He wasn't the cleverest of people, Divy, and Tek Life broke into his grimy flat and found him asleep on a mattress on the floor with a young girl. The gun had been left in a plastic bag, by the mattress, next to a load of cocaine. By the time the police had arrived, the girl, the drugs and Patrick had gone. The only person the police found was Divy, handcuffed to a chair in his boxer shorts, sobbing like a little girl.

Sean and Divy gave up everyone involved: Kully, Dee and Busta. Elliot came over the second night after Jas died and told us the news. She went through everything that Sean and Divy had told them and then admitted that Busta had been given a light sentence in return for becoming an informer. I went mad then, snapping out of shock.

'And you told us we could trust you,' I spat at her.

'You can—' she replied, trying to calm me down.

'Fuck off! You gave that nonce no time at all and then let him do what he did. Jas wouldn't be dead if you hadn't – he wouldn't be dead!'

Elliot came over and sat on the arm of my chair. She shook her head and put a hand on my shoulder. 'Jas was trying to petrol-bomb your house — we *know* that. I'm sorry about Busta but we didn't know what he was doing to you. No one did.'

'An' yuh gwan let him off again,' asked Nanny, steely-eyed.

'No,' whispered Elliot. 'This time he gets his full due — I'm going to make sure of it. My new boss is with me on this, too.'

'Why the fuck should we believe a thing you say?' I asked, but I didn't wait for her reply.

I got up, wiped my eyes and went for a walk, trying to get my head round the fact that Jas had been trying to kill us when he'd set himself on fire. That and the fact that I had a brother, Tyrone, who had helped Divy set us up. Not that I'd told the police anything about his involvement. Divy and Busta had conned him just like they'd conned everyone else. And the police were far from being my favourite people. I walked up the main road and over to the precinct, with my head full of these thoughts. I stopped outside Mr Singh's off-licence and went in and bought myself a can of strong lager. Then I went and sat on one of the bollards and had a drink, just like I used to do when I was thirteen — only back then Jas would be sitting opposite me, chatting nonsense about how many girls he had dealt with.

When I got back, Elliot had gone and everyone was asleep part from Ellie and Nanny, who were in the kitchen. Ellie gave me a hug when I walked in and then kissed me.

'You OK?' she asked.

'No,' I said honestly. 'I'm just . . . I can't . . .'

'I know,' she said.

Nanny sat down at the table and let out a sigh. 'Time ago heal,' he told us. 'Right now yuh feel raw like when yuh cut yuhself. But de skin ago grow back, Jah know.'

I shrugged. 'Will it?' I asked, not sure that it would.

'One day,' replied Nanny, lighting a spliff. 'Yuh can't stop de sun from rise, my yout'.'

END

I walked over to Lynden and Tyrone and smiled.

'You all right?' I asked.

'Cool,' replied my dad.

'How 'bout you?' I asked my brother.

He shrugged. 'I'm just sorry,' he said sadly.

'I know,' I replied. 'I'm sorry too but I didn't do this and neither did you, really.'

'Yeah,' he said. 'I did. I should have checked it out – seen what was goin' on and that.'

'Maybe we all should have,' I told him. 'I'll see you around, bro.'

Tyrone nodded. 'If that's OK,' he replied.

'Yeah – it is,' I said.

I left them at the entrance to the crematorium and joined the Crew. Will and Della were holding hands, talking quietly, and Ellie was watching me. I put my hand in hers and gave her a kiss.

'This feels so weird,' I told her.

'What does?' she asked me.

'All of this – funerals and speaking to a brother I never knew I had. And going out with you.'

Her face fell. 'Is it a problem now?' she asked.

I shook my head.

'No – it's just that I don't know where I am at the moment,' I told her.

'You're here with me,' she replied. 'And with Will and Della and our families and friends.'

I smiled and kissed her again. In my head I could hear Jas ripping me over it.

'*Man, I always told you she was on yer case. Chatting 'bout yuh nuh fancy her. Look at you now, bro – loved up.*'

'Like I am – yuh chat shit, you know that?' I replied.

Ellie looked at me like I was crazy. 'Who you talkin' to?' she asked.

I shrugged. 'Jas,' I told her. 'Just one last time . . .'

ABOUT THE AUTHOR

Bali Rai lives in Leicester and his days of working behind a bar and thinking about becoming a journalist are a distant memory. He now gets out of bed nice and early, mostly to write and increasingly to visit schools all over the country to talk about his books. If he's really lucky, he's heading for the airport to go and speak in exciting places all over Europe, as the nice people are still inviting him.

His mum still thinks he should get a proper job, and a wife, but there are too many Liverpool FC matches on Sky to think about organising a wedding in the near future.

The Whisper is his fourth novel for Corgi. Its prequel, *The Crew*, won two regional book awards. His debut novel, *(un)arranged marriage*, also won four book awards.

THE CREW

When you live in the concrete heart of a major UK city and someone leaves a bag full of cash in the alley behind your house you had best leave it alone. It's got to be bad news – after all, what kind of people leave fifteen grand lying around?

Winner of the *Leicester Book Award* and the *Calderdale Book Award*.

0 552 54739 5

RANI & SUKH

Rani and Sukh have just started going out together. But Rani is a Sandhu and Sukh is a Bains – and sometimes names can lead to serious trouble . . . A gripping novel that sweeps the reader from modern-day Britain to the Punjab in the 1960s and back again in a ceaseless cycle of tragedy and conflict.

'Frustratingly honest and overwhelmingly powerful' *The Bookseller*

Shortlisted for the *Booktrust Teenage Prize* and three regional book awards.

0 552 54890 1

(UN)ARRANGED MARRIAGE

Manny is a Punjabi boy from Leicester and he doesn't want to get married . . . A stunning debut novel about generational gulfs and cultural differences within family and society.

'Absorbing and engaging . . . a highly readable debut from Bali Rai that teenagers of any culture will identify with' *Observer*

Winner of the *Angus Book Award*, the *Leicester Book Award*, the *Stockport Schools Award* and the *North Lanarkshire Catalyst Book Award*. Shortlisted for the *Branford Boase Award* and four regional literature awards.

0 552 54734 4